GONE TO WAR

Vol. Three of New Mexico Gal

ENID E. HAAG

WestBow Press
A DIVISION OF THOMAS NELSON
& ZONDERVAN

Copyright © 2018 Enid E. Haag.

All rights reserved. No part of this book may be used or reproduced by any means, graphic, electronic, or mechanical, including photocopying, recording, taping or by any information storage retrieval system without the written permission of the author except in the case of brief quotations embodied in critical articles and reviews.

This is a work of fiction. All of the characters, names, incidents, organizations, and dialogue in this novel are either the products of the author's imagination or are used fictitiously.

WestBow Press books may be ordered through booksellers or by contacting:

WestBow Press
A Division of Thomas Nelson & Zondervan
1663 Liberty Drive
Bloomington, IN 47403
www.westbowpress.com
1 (866) 928-1240

Because of the dynamic nature of the Internet, any web addresses or links contained in this book may have changed since publication and may no longer be valid. The views expressed in this work are solely those of the author and do not necessarily reflect the views of the publisher, and the publisher hereby disclaims any responsibility for them.

Any people depicted in stock imagery provided by Getty Images are models, and such images are being used for illustrative purposes only. Certain stock imagery © Getty Images.

ISBN: 978-1-9736-2873-6 (sc)
ISBN: 978-1-9736-2874-3 (hc)
ISBN: 978-1-9736-2872-9 (e)

Library of Congress Control Number: 2018905901

Print information available on the last page.

WestBow Press rev. date: 5/31/2018

In memory of the women

who served with the Army Nurse Corps during World War I.

May their service and sacrifice never be forgotten.

Acknowledgments

Many thanks to Jonathan Casey, Archivist at the Edward Jones Research Center at the National WWI Museum and Memorial in Kansas City, Missouri for all his assistance in locating and providing primary sources regarding the WWI Army Nurse Corp, especially the letters and diary of Alta Andrews Sharp pictured on the cover. Alta Sharp from Elgin, Illinois, served in the Army Nurse Corps in France during WWI. Her letters were invaluable in confirming and substantiating historical facts concerning experiences of American nurses.

It is with heartfelt thanks that I remember Lee Hanson, who read several of the revisions of the manuscript and offered many wise suggestions before her unexpected death 1 September, 2017. I am truly sorry she will not see the published book.

I thank Joanne and Vice Admiral M. Staser Holcomb USN (ret) who read and made suggestions on the early chapters dealing with the Atlantic onboard crossing with a Naval convoy.

Many thanks to the Rev. Richard Weyls, St. Andrew's Episcopal Church, Seattle, WA. for his explanation of Roman Catholic practices and a wonderful story suggestion regarding the rosery.

Evelyn Nordeen, thank you for answering my many questions regarding nursing in general. Your patience with my inquisitives was much appreciated.

Finally, special nods go to Lillie Day and Liza Biscomb for their encouragement, support, and proofreading of the manuscript.

Preface

Gone to War is the last volume in the *New Mexico Gal* trilogy, a family saga covering the life of Emma from 1906 to 1919. The first volume, *Gone to Texas,* begins when ten-year-old Emma is separated from her family in the great San Francisco earthquake. Rescued by Enrico Caruso, she's reunites with her Spanish American New Mexico relatives and slowly begins to recover from the trauma of the loss of her family. Because of cultural prejudices and family secrets, the court awarded custody of Emma to her Texas uncle, placing her in an untenable family situation. After many adventures and growing friendship with a neighbor boy, Wolfe, Emma is reunited with her father. The second volume, *Gone to Idaho,* continues teenage Emma's story as she follows her father to Idaho in search of her mother. Emma's two friends, Juan and Wolfe, travel with her through Colorado and Idaho, creating a teen love triangle that is carried on in this final volume of the trilogy. The second volume introduces Jamie, who rescues Emma's mother from a flaming building in San Francisco, and who also serves as her guardian until she recovers from amnesia and is reunited with Emma's father. This final volume of the trilogy is the story of adult Emma in her early twenties serving in the Army Nurse Corps during World War I in France. The volume is self-contained so that readers do not have to have read the first two to follow the story line.

1

Only the sound of steps on wooden planks revealed the presence of the nurses walking single file along the army's port of embarkation in Hoboken, New Jersey. Their exact whereabouts were a mystery to a westerner like Emma, except she knew she was close to New York City. The soft lapping of water against the dock heightened her apprehension of the forthcoming ocean voyage. Other than a few hours rafting as a child with Wolfe, now her fiancé, on the Guadalupe River in Texas, she'd never sailed on anything as large as the ship she was about to board.

Germany had started all-out war on shipping between the United States and Europe. Although she knew they would be traveling in a convoy protected by armed merchant and naval vessels, she knew they faced the chance of being torpedoed by German submarines. Recently, the newspapers had been filled with reports of many ships, not just American, being torpedoed along the coast of France, in the English Channel, and even along the New England seaboard. That knowledge didn't bring comfort to anyone traveling the Atlantic Ocean, and certainly not to Emma.

Moving forward, she shook off her apprehension and concentrated on how fortunate she was; she'd finally made it to the point that she was actually headed to France. When war erupted in 1914 in Europe, England's appeal for trained nurses awakened Emma's desire to volunteer. She knew she was qualified. She was unmarried, between the ages of twenty-five and thirty-five, Caucasian, and a graduate of a training school. It had taken several interviews before she was accepted into the Army Nurse Corps legislated by Congress in 1902. She was ordered first to the base hospital at Fort Bliss in El Paso, Texas, for training. That was where she learned to wake up to the sound of a bugle, learned how military medical services differed from civilian, and learned how to distinguish between an officer and an enlisted man.

While at Fort Bliss, she enjoyed the companionship of Juan, her New Mexico childhood buddy who was a nephew of her aunt Maria. Juan, an officer in the Veterinary Corps, arranged on weekends for them to go horseback riding, something they both enjoyed. Once Emma got used to the English saddle with its very low pommel, which the army preferred over the cavalry saddle, her stress level evaporated. The two happily explored the many rocky and slightly hilly trails on Fort Bliss as they laughed and shared hilarious events experienced during the week.

Her next orders sent Emma to the station hospital at Fort Sam Houston in San Antonio, Texas, where she was issued her uniforms and other necessities. Before receiving her orders to proceed to New York City, she spent several weeks receiving training on different wards.

Emma's last name, Roeder, identified her as being of German descent. During the two and a half years between England's entry into the war and the United States declaring war, prejudice toward people of German descent appeared all over the country. Many citizens questioned the loyalty of German Americans, including some of her coworkers who were suspicious of her. She'd even experienced some bias during her interview to enter the Army Nurse Corps.

While in Texas, she learned that many recent immigrants clung to their German cultural heritage and language. She was surprised to learn that some sent money to support their former fatherland and hoped that her papa's family in New Braunfels didn't do this.

Prejudice against all things German became ridiculous when people refused to eat foods deemed "unpatriotic" because of their names, such as German chocolate cake and German potato salad; even sauerkraut was renamed "liberty cabbage." *How laughable,* Emma thought. Violence had increased against German Americans. Even speaking German in public was prohibited, as was the teaching of German language in schools. Emma congratulated herself that she never learned much of the language.

One afternoon while sightseeing in San Antonio, Emma watched as a German-named street sign was replaced by an Anglo American one. She found the loyalty of her fellow German Americans to the country they immigrated from disheartening and difficult to understand, having grown up in the multicultural community of Santa Fe. Fortunately, on one of her visits to New Braunfels, she discovered that her relatives there, as well as the community, shared her allegiance to their new homeland: America.

While Emma was stationed at Fort Sam's station hospital, Captain Dora E. Thompson, fourth superintendent of the Army Nurse Corps, visited. Emma learned that the captain's first assignment after joining the army in 1902 had been at the Presidio in San Francisco during the earthquake in 1906. Emma's father, mother, and brother disappeared in the disaster, leaving her orphaned for a time. When Emma visited with Captain Dora, she was overjoyed at finding someone who could fill in for her what really had happened on that fateful day because, as a ten-year-old, her memory was hazy. Captain Dora, after learning of Emma's loss, explained how many people like her brother went missing and were never found. She'd been fortunate that she'd eventually been reunited with her parents.

At Fort Sam, Emma's round of assignments included the general surgical ward. During her first week there, all the nurses and corpsmen on the ward came down with a bug except Emma, who at once visited a pharmacy to purchase a bottle of castor oil that she liberally imbibed. Her quick thinking and action resulted in her joining everyone else in throwing up and experiencing diarrhea, so she wasn't accused of being a saboteur and trying to poison anyone. Those were charges many good German Americans faced, including some doctors.

In the fall of 1917, Emma received orders for duty in France. She'd traveled by train along with several nurses from San Antonio to New York City, where they joined others from all over the country at the Holly Hotel, also referred to by many as the Holly Inn. Once an elegant three-story Victorian structure with a tower, a fire in 1912 demolished the tower but the remaining building remained as a landmark in the community. In this stylish abode, Emma and her fellow nurses waited to board a ship to take them first to England and then over to France.

Informed after meeting their newly assigned chief nurse that they'd march in a parade down Fifth Avenue before boarding their ship, their excitement at being in New York City, a first-time experience for many, was dampened by the thought of marching. Taking temperatures and giving shots they knew how to do, but marching in a big parade? Would they make fools of themselves?

Early on the morning of the parade, the chief nurse rousted them from their beds, ordering them outside before even having breakfast. She handed them over to an army sergeant who lined them up in rows and marched them back and forth, all the while yelling at the ones who got out of step. Some who couldn't tell left from right were given rocks to carry in their right hands to help them. Over and over they marched, turning corners with some failing to turn in the correct direction. "You look terrible! You're a disgrace to the army!" shouted the sergeant.

Pretty soon, it was time to join the parade. They stood grim faced and listened. "Don't you dare look at anything but the person in front of you. Remember nurses don't faint, so don't. Or you'll be on the next train home. Do the Army Nurse Corps proud," said the chief nurse as she took her position in front to lead with the sergeant as guidon bearer and another man at the rear to pick up the fallen. They stepped out with the chief nurse in the lead, staring straight ahead. They marched smartly in their newly issued, bulky, yellow, leather Coward boots. No one fainted, no one saw the cheering crowd, but they did hear them.

And everyone made it to the end of the parade.

With no lights allowed near the dock, Emma walked behind the shadowy figure of the person ahead. Even though she'd followed the suggestion of the chief nurse at Fort Sam and spent hours attempting to break in her new Coward shoes, which were more like men's work boots than shoes, the effort to soften the leather failed. They'd chafed every soft and boney spot of her now complaining feet. Her feet throbbed.

The rest period allocated to them after the parade and bus ride to the New Jersey dock had been a godsend, but there was not sufficient time to ease her fussing feet. Only her bladder. The shoes were one of two pairs issued to her, along with a blue, serge uniform, two hats, four gray chambray everyday uniforms, twelve butcher's aprons, white collars and cuffs, a blue, silk blouse and a white, poplin one, woolen hose and tights, underwear, a bathrobe, and flannelette pajamas, two gray sweaters, rubber boots, a poncho, a dark-blue overcoat, a raincoat, and a wool sleeping bag. Her aching arm reminded her she'd also received smallpox, typhoid, and paratyphoid vaccinations. Around her neck hung her very own circular dog tag like all the soldiers had. She'd also been issued an official army identification card.

Waiting to have her name ticked off the boarding list, Emma

couldn't help thinking back about her last days at home in Santa Fe. She especially recalled her bedroom that had served as a haven while waiting for orders to report for duty. A smile flickered across her face as she visualized Fiver, her precious calico cat and loyal confidant. He seemed to sense her impending departure and followed her everywhere as she moved about sorting belongings to store or to take with her. The little minx had even tried hiding in her duffle bag by trying to wrap himself in her panties but only succeeded in getting his head stuck in a leg hole! She could still feel his soft, wet nose on her cheek and hear his loud purr as she released him from his entanglement. "Sorry, old fellow, the Army doesn't allow pets." Before her departure while rubbing his tummy, she instructed him to keep the house free of vermin, especially mice, and not let any into their bedroom.

With some misgiving, she reminisced about having to exchange her St. Joseph's nurse's cap that identified her as one of their graduates, for the Army issued one so very plain, which only distinguished her as a nurse. With nostalgia, she recalled her capping ceremony just six months into her training at St. Joseph's Hospital in Albuquerque. Along with eight of her classmates in starch white dresses reaching just above their ankles covered by blue-and-white-striped aprons indicating they were students, she'd marched down the aisle of the chapel carrying her recently handmade cap and a replica of the Nightingale lamp. A smile flickered across her face as she remembered struggling to shape the fabric pieces given her into a cap using tiny stitches. Thank goodness Aunt Maria, while visiting, came to her rescue, taking the cap apart, redoing it properly so she wouldn't be ashamed. On a visit home, she'd taken fabric and the pattern with her so her aunt could make a spare. Now she wouldn't be wearing either one until war's end and her return to civilian life.

For the capping ceremony, every parent and friend who

could travel to Albuquerque, including Mama and Jamie, her stepfather, stood as the student nurses progressed toward Sister Mary Katherine, who stood at the railing in front of the small hospital chapel altar. One by one, as each student's name was called, they knelt in front of Sister and had their cap placed on their head. Remaining kneeing, they repeated together the Florence Nightingale Pledge.

> *I solemnly pledge myself before God and in the presence of this assembly, to pass my life in purity and to practise my profession faithfully. I will abstain from whatever is deleterious and mischievous, and will not take or knowingly administer any harmful drug. I will do all in my power to maintain and elevate the standard of my profession, and will hold in confidence all personal matters committed to my keeping, and all family affairs coming to my knowledge in the practice of my calling. With loyalty will I endeavour to aid the physician in his work, and as a 'missioner of health' I will dedicate myself to devoted service to human welfare.*

A push from behind roused Emma from her thoughts. The line was moving forward, not much, but a few steps. She glanced up at the hulk of the ship beside her that would be her home for the next twelve to fourteen days. Hopefully, their quarters would be heated, unlike the one assigned them when they arrived at San Antonio, where the heat hadn't been turned on until their bus pulled up in front of the barracks. Shivering from remembering how very chilly that first night had been with the icy sheets and one thin wool blanket on the Army cot, Emma pulled her coat front tighter together. It wasn't easy because she'd layered one of her sweaters on under the coat to save space in her duffle. Like all the other nurses, she'd also pulled on an extra pair of woolen hose after hearing that replacements might be unavailable in France.

When she reached the security guards, her military identification card was scrutinized first by an Army sergeant and then a naval policeman before she was allowed to start up the gang plank to the ship. As she stepped aboard, she was handed a slip of paper. "Don't lose this," said a croaky voice obviously needing rest. "It's your billet sheet assigning you to where you'll sleep during the voyage."

"Ma'am, if you will follow me, I'll direct you to your berthing area," said a youngish sailor leading the way to a door where he directed her, "Follow the others." Ahead, she recognized her fellow nurses and followed them down the inside stairs and along a hall into a large space crowded with bunks.

"Wow, if they haven't dumped us in steerage!" exclaimed someone.

"What did you think?" came a retort. "Did you expect first-class accommodations?"

"No, this looks like second class renovated to transport as many bodies as necessary over to France," came an answer.

Newly constructed wooden bunk beds, one on top of another, row upon row, adjacent to the narrow aisle for people to access their bunks, made Emma claustrophobic as she stepped sideways in the dimly lighted space looking for her berth number.

Stacked on each bunk lay folded sheets, a blanket, and a pillow. Emma heard someone sigh, "And we have our beds to make too." Shaking her head, Emma, silently agreed.

"Just be glad we have a place to lay our heads."

Later, they learned they were traveling on the former passenger ship the *Finland,* one of thirteen privately owned American passenger ships now under the authority of the U.S. government to transport troops across to France. The ship had been chosen because it could make the transatlantic crossing without refueling, plus it had been at an American port when the United States declared war on the German Empire on April 1917.

Both the second- and third-class interiors of the *Finland* had been ripped out and fitted to accommodate almost twice the original number of intended passengers. Although the nurses were in the Army, they had no military rank and were lucky to be assigned the second-class accommodations for their trip across to England.

After dumping her duffle bag near her berth, Emma and the other nurses scurried up to the dining area carrying their life jackets. After all were assembled, they were instructed on how to put their jackets on in case of an emergency. Since it was nighttime, they would receive further safety procedures in the morning. For now, they were discharged to go to their quarters.

2

The first night, despite being assigned a top berth, Emma found the space comfortable but confining, with insufficient room to turn over so she could lie on her side. Thank goodness, she usually slept on her back. Getting into the bunk had taken an act of Houdini! All those in the upper berths giggled as they tried different antics to climb up and slide into the space. "Thank goodness, we're all young and physically fit," chuckled Emma to no one in particular.

Pitch blackness engulfed the quarters when the lights were turned off, but on that first night, exhaustion from the day's events quickly caught up with everyone. Even the sounds of breathing and snoring of her sister nurses in random rhythm with the ships hum didn't keep Emma awake. If she'd been in a first-class cabin between silk sheets, she didn't think she'd have slept any sounder. Even her mind, which usually would have raced with visions of being torpedoed to floating in the ocean with nothing to keep her afloat, didn't deep-six her slumber.

Morning found Emma dressing in half light, jockeying with everyone else for footing in the aisle as the ship pitched and lurched. Swaying from side to side, she finally queued at the entrance to the toilet area because, although they'd increased the number of facilities, there still wasn't enough to accommodate the number of females and their toiletry needs. As she waited her turn, some pushed their way forward, pale faced and holding hands to mouths seeking a toilet for immediate relief. No one had told them that nurses couldn't be seasick! They just couldn't faint!

The first order of the day was more safety instruction, including reporting to their assigned life boat stations in case of having to abandon ship. Shivering from standing on the rolling deck and buffeted by an icy wind, they were finally dismissed for breakfast. Everyone rushed below, crowding in line for hot coffee. Emma clasped her mug with both hands to warm her numb fingers and stomped her feet. Eagerly, she took a sip of the welcoming liquid from her mug only to realize too late that it was so hot, and she burned her tongue. The startling hot coffee spilled onto her hand, eliciting a "OZXJW!"

"Haven't you heard, Emma? Nurses don't swear," said a bemused nurse standing next to her.

Nodding, as she slid her tray along, Emma watched as toast landed on the plate on her tray along with a large glob of yellow fluff with reddish/brown flakes. Looking up at the server, she asked, "What's that?"

She heard a grunt, "Egg and corn beef. What did you expect, eggs Benedict?"

Oh, she thought, *what I wouldn't do for rancheros like Aunt Maria makes at home.* Her mouth puckered with the thought of green chili as she looked down at her food. *Perhaps a squirt of catsup will help,* she thought as she slid into the first vacant seat. Glancing sideways, she saw everyone scooping up their breakfast with relish and spreading raspberry jam on the cold burnt toast. Ignoring the jam, Emma dunked her toast in her coffee and downed her mystery egg concoction to calm her complaining stomach, even though her taste buds failed to register any flavor whatsoever.

"Attention! Please remain seated after you've eaten," called the Chief Nurse, standing midway in the dining area. "The ship's captain is going to talk to us. I'll call 'attention' when he arrives. Please stand up until he says, 'At ease,' at which time you may be seated."

Slowly, the buzzing of conversation resumed. Emma sipped the remaining coffee left in her mug and turned to the person beside her. "I thought we'd been given all our instructions earlier this morning out on the freezing deck."

"Guess not. Be thankful we're inside. I've had a hard time remaining upright. We're rolling and pitching so. I hope I don't get seasick like some," said her companion, who spoke with a western twang.

Just then there was commotion at the door. Walking into the mess, a sober-faced, strikingly handsome male wearing starched bluish dungaree trousers and shirt appeared. "Attention!" called out the Chief Nurse. Chair legs groaned as they scraped the floor, metal trays slid into each other, and a few muffled giggles escaped.

"At ease." After all were seated and the noise subsided, "Good morning, ladies!" said the officer in front of them. "Thank you. I'm Captain Willing, senior Navy officer on board. You are sailing on the refurbished *Finland* manned by merchant officers and crew, along with naval officers and men here to provide protection should the ship come under attack. The ship is traveling in a convoy as a defense against the German submarines during our transatlantic voyage. Throughout the trip, we will be sailing a zigzag course to avoid attack. This shouldn't cause you any trouble except for maybe upset stomachs until you adjust to it or fall out of bed because of it. So be careful as you walk about. During the day, I urge you to keep a hand on the railings at all times, being especially careful when using the stairs. The *Finland* is manned with a Navy gunnery crew. Should we come under attack, for your own protection, please remain below unless you hear five long blasts on the ship's horn followed by another five blasts, at which time proceed topside to your assigned life boat station. Wear your life jackets at all times and keep them under your pillow at night, readily available in an emergency. You may even wish to wear them while you sleep as a cushion, should you be slung out of bed because of the zigzagging. I will try to make this voyage as pleasant and uneventful as possible. I know you've heard this during your training, but let me remind you that there is to be no fraternization with the civilian crew or noncommissioned officers. Are there any questions?"

From the back came, "So there's two captains on board, one civilian and one military. Why?"

"Good question. The civilian crew and captain worked on the *Finland* before our government recommissioned the ship for military service. We need their help in operating the ship because the Navy doesn't, as of yet, have the manpower to take total control of all the ships needed to transport a fighting force to France. The few of us in the Navy that are aboard take over only in case we're attacked—that's our expertise."

"So you'll be in command whenever we're under attack?" came a shout from the back of the room.

"That's correct."

"What do you suppose we do with all the time on our hands?" questioned the jesting nurse sitting next to Emma. "Practice our bandaging techniques or, better yet, perfect the art of bloodletting on the boys aboard?"

Turning toward her jovial partner with a mischievous look, Emma answered, "Better still, let's practice our patient skills such as bathing and shaving." As both grinned at their lighthearted quips, she stretched out her hand, saying, "I'm Emma Roeder from Santa Fe, New Mexico."

"I'm Jackie McBride from Denver, Colorado, your neighbor to the north. Nice to meet a fellow westerner. I don't think there's many of us in our group who are."

"Were you sent to Fort Sam Houston or Fort Bliss?"

"I went directly to Fort Sam," answered Jackie. "Most of us from Colorado did. Don't know why. Fort Bliss was closer and I would have liked to have seen El Paso. It sounds so exotic."

"You didn't miss a thing. They kept us so busy we hardly had any time to sightsee. Anyway, Mexico was off-limits because of the recent fighting between our two counties. We didn't even get time to get off the post."

As the two started to leave the table, they heard others dividing into fours for bridge. "Are you a cardplayer?" Asked Jackie.

Emma shook her head. "No, I've never had time for cards. When I wasn't working at the store or studying, I practiced my violin. How about you?"

Giving a chuckle, Jackie answered, "I'm a meathead as far as cards are concerned. Never can remember what I played or for that matter what the cards are named."

As they walked back toward their assigned bunks, Emma pulled out her billet sheet to jog her memory as to which bunk was hers. "I don't want to crawl into the wrong bunk. They all look alike."

"Oh dear!" exclaimed Jackie as she stopped in the aisle. "I don't have my billet sheet with me. I was in such a rush to get to breakfast …"

"Hey, you two, keep going or stand aside so the rest of us can get through."

Chagrined at having created an obstruction, Emma pulled Jackie onto the nearest lower bunk. "Oh, wait a minute," chuckled Jackie, "I think this is my bunk. "Here's my long johns peeking out from the pillow." Bursting into laughter, the two made themselves comfortable at either end of the berth, drawing their legs up so they sat cross-legged facing each other. As the morning progressed, they learned that each had received their nurse's training under the auspices of the Sisters of Charity at hospitals both named St. Joseph's.

"I had wanted to go to the University of Texas Medical Branch School of Nursing in Austin," commented Emma, "originally known as the John Sealy Hospital Training School for Nurses. My New Braunfels side of the family was looking forward to my being close to them. When I looked into the requirements for acceptance, I discovered I didn't qualify."

Jackie nodded, "Me too. I wanted to go back east to the John Hopkins Hospital Training School for Nurses so I could work under the famous Isabel Robb but couldn't get in."

"Lucky for us, many of the locally operated hospitals offered nursing programs. Did you get to stay at home, Jackie, or did they require you to live at the nurses' dorm?"

Shifting her legs from beneath her, Jackie answered, "All the nursing students had to live in the dorm. Didn't you?"

Emma straightened her legs, winced, then stood up, reaching down to the calf of her right leg to rub out a cramp from sitting so long. "Sure, we had to live in the dorm. Between classes and working on the wards, they ran us off our feet. I think we were the 'in-betweens' as far as schooling was concerned. I've read that formal book-learning nursing education is now out of favor for the more practical experience kind that we received," Emma said, taking some deep knee bends in an effort to get the feeling back in her legs. "Want to join me in some exercise?"

Both girls began to walk in place and take a few deep knee bends. Before long, they made funny faces at each other while laughing at their antics. Soon other nurses around them joined in the exercise session and girlish giggles rang throughout. First one and then another introduced a different exercise to try in the aisle. Cheers erupted as first one and then another fell onto a bunk as the ship pitched with a zigzag movement.

3

Catastrophe struck not many hours out from the New York harbor! Emma watched one after another of the nurses throw up and take to their bunks. Between the constant motion and the zigzagging of the ship to avoid attack, it was understandable that some got sick—even the merchant sailors did! They'd never zigzagged while sailing. Emma, along with a couple other nurses after experiencing the beginnings of nausea recovered with no ill effects except for short periods of queasiness whenever the ship abruptly zagged more than usual. One of the naval officers remarked at breakfast that they zigzagged only every one and a half minutes. *Impossible,* thought Emma. *Would they keep this up all the way to England? Ridiculous!*

The dozen nurses unaffected by the seasickness organized themselves into shifts to care for their bedridden sisters, including the Chief Nurse who had been one of the first to be stricken. They emptied makeshift spittoons made from used ten-gallon cans from the galley, washed faces, and kept dampened cloths on foreheads. There's no cure for seasickness except patience and time. Preventing dehydration is essential, so encouraging sips of weak tea took on the appearance of a watering brigade. Thankfully, the ship's steward rigged up a large kettle of tea that was kept at one end of the room so they wouldn't have to traipse all the way to the dining hall and back. Once recovery started, nourishment was needed, so plates of biscuits appeared along with the tea. The ship's steward knew his business. Almost half the trip was over before the nurses had recovered enough to take their meals in the dining room, including the Chief Nurse, who never again lectured them, "Nurses, don't get sick."

During the seasickness episode, the unaffected nurses exchanged personal stories. The one who kept them laughing the most was Ann Nelson from Seattle, Washington. When the Chief Nurse succumbed to the seasickness, she commented with a straight face, "Nurses don't get sick, you know, not even Chief Nurses." That brought laughter to the table and quizzical looks from the male officers seated nearby. Ann elaborated, "When she applied to nursing school the first time, she was refused because she admitted being sick during her monthlies. At her next interview, when asked about her health, she replied she was as healthy as a horse. She got accepted into the nursing program."

Nell Crystal shared what her family doctor told her to say when she applied: "Emphasize you have had all the childhood diseases!" She never admitted being prone to catching every cold or flu bug.

"Why do they expect us to be superhuman and never get sick? That's crazy!"

"Well, we've gone a long way to proving we are superhuman, at least for all the nursing we've done over the past week," smiled Ann, as she got up to bus her tray, taking the long way around so she could flirt with a good-looking young naval officer.

As people began to regain their strength, Emma and the others who had helped nurse those back to health were able to return to a normal schedule themselves. Emma especially enjoyed taking advantage of her allotted time to walk around the deck for fresh air, even though she needed to layer her clothing against the wind. On one such outing, she walked alone, enjoying some personal thinking time. After circling the deck ten times, her toes as well as her fingers began to complain. She decided to end her exercise but when she tried to pull the door open to go inside, she couldn't budge it even after several attempts. Looking around, she spied a young Army officer approaching, head down against the wind. Afraid he might not see her predicament, she grabbed his arm and pointed to the door. Nodding his understanding, he too struggled before being able to open the door. "Thank you. I could have frozen out there if you hadn't come along," she said.

"Glad to be of service," smiled the young officer. Holding out his hand toward her, he added, "I'm Lieutenant Ben Zeiger. Those doors are really heavy and with the wind blowing against them even harder than usual to pull open."

She stripped her gloves off to rub feeling back into her fingers. "That door was quite impossible for me and I'm fairly strong. I'll not walk alone again for getting back in."

"A cup of coffee would warm us up. Would you care to join me?"

Walking side by side to the dining hall, Emma, glancing discreetly, noticed that Ben walked double jointed. He towered over her by more than a foot but was lean, almost gaunt. He'd removed his cap upon entering the dining hall, revealing a mop of unruly dark brown hair matching his bushy eyebrows that offset the lightest of blue eyes.

They filled their mugs and took two vacant seats at a table where a couple of officers were deep in thought over a chessboard.

All passengers where restricted to the ship's interior during the daylight hours, except for their allocated deck time. Going outside at night was strictly forbidden for fear of alerting an enemy ship or sub. The dining hall therefore represented the "R & R," rest and recreation center during the day for everyone but closed by 2100 hours because of the "lights out" restriction.

During the day, except during meals, the dining hall provided entertainment organized by a civilian staff. People could find just about everything to amuse themselves: games such as Monopoly or card games, people singing around the piano, dancing in a cleared space, knitters sitting in a circle chatting together, wood carvers comparing techniques, and people reading the books from the library book boxes provided by volunteer groups. The ship's steward kept a large coffee urn filled and plates of biscuits to keep the troops' thoughts off of where the trip was taking them.

Despite the voices around them, Emma and Ben talked between sips of coffee and bites of ginger biscuits. Both shared that they were engaged, Ben to a girl waiting back home in Crete, Nebraska, and Emma to Wolfe, already serving in France. Ben divulged to Emma that he was attached to General "Black Jack" Pershing's staff, and he remembered traveling through New Braunfels, Texas, via the train on their way to the Mexico–New Mexico border to fight Pancho Villa. Emma shared that her cousin Juan had been at Columbus, New Mexico, during the raid and had been injured. "Funny how our paths meet even when we're from different states," she remarked. "My father grew up in New Braunfels and I spent a few years staying with family there until my father recovered from his injuries from the San Francisco earthquake."

For the next hour, Ben insisted Emma tell of her experiences during and after the 1906 California earthquake. It wasn't long before a group gathered around their table listening to her describe the humorous side of the opera star Caruso, who many had personally seen perform.

Howls of laughter erupted when she told of her two friends Jean and Wolfe on horseback jumping from the cattle car down into a herd of unruly livestock surrounding the train, preventing it from moving along the track. Their added mounted manpower assisted the beleaguered cowboys to maneuver the beasties away from the tracks, allowing the train to continue on its way.

During another coffee break, Emma learned that Ben, a first-generation American, had attended the University of Nebraska with a football scholarship. His time playing football was cut short by a knee injury that the doctor thought would be permanent but turned out not to be, thanks to the skillful hands of the team's trainer, Jack Best. Ben ended up in the Nebraska National Guard, which helped him pay for college and also introduced him to Pershing, who lead the unit down to the Mexican border skirmish. When President Wilson called on General Pershing to take over command of the American Expeditionary Force, he recruited Ben to be part of his command.

Looking at Ben, Emma's eyes sparkled with admiration. "I'll bet your parents are so proud of you."

"They are, as is the whole family. As you know from your own experience, times have been rough since 1914 for us German Americans. There's so much prejudice against us because of our culture, our language, our literature, and even our music, but in Nebraska, things have turned around a lot. Many of us are serving in divisions nicknamed the Fighting Farmers, the Rainbow Division, and the Middlewest Division. No one should question our loyalty to our country."

Their conversation continued until the steward and his staff began to place dinner out for the approaching meal. "Shall we guess what we're having?" jested Emma, now feeling comfortable enough with her new acquaintance to tease.

Getting up from their seats, they headed for the line already assembled around the length of the room. Laughingly raising his nose in the air so he could pretend a whiff, "Aw, my favorite, corn beef hash from the great state of Nebraska."

"Pipe down, Nebraska—we've heard enough about your great state's contribution to the war effort."

Turning toward the speaker, who Ben knew was from Kansas, he said, "Look who's bellyaching, a Jayhawk whose team always loses to the Nebraska Cornhuskers."

The friendly banter quieted down as people began to eat with newly made friends. The Army nurses sat with the a few Red Cross nurses but separate from the women attached to the Salvation Army, YWCA, and other civilian volunteers. Emma expected the Salvation Army and YWCA to send volunteers across, but the number of women secretaries, telephone operators, ambulance drivers, bacteriologist, dietitians, and librarians surprised her. There were more of them than nurses! And she'd learned from one of the nurses whose sister volunteered as a telephone operator that they earned more per month than the nurses did, whose pay was ninety dollars a month. Emma consoled herself that she didn't join for the money. *I came because I wanted to do my duty*, she thought.

Emma glanced at Jackie. Dark complexioned, sharped nosed, and black short curly haired, Jackie struck Emma as a strong individual, self-sufficient and dependable; she sat across the table next to their new acquaintance Maddie, who'd recently graduated from a nursing program in Texas.

"What enticed you to sign up for the Army Nurse Corps, Maddie?"

"Well, like you all, I wanted to serve my country, but also, I'm looking for my brother. He's somewhere in Germany," she confided.

"How did he end up in Germany?"

Maddie looked around the women sitting near her before speaking. "My German grandmother fell and broke her hip. Instead of sending her to a nursing home, my oldest brother decided to go over to Germany to care for her until he could bring her back to Texas. Before she recovered enough to travel, Kurt found himself conscripted into the German Army."

"Couldn't he prove he was an American citizen?" asked Jackie.

"No, that was just it. Kurt didn't have anything official declaring him a citizen, and even though every villager vouched for him, nothing helped. He neglected to take his birth certificate with him to Germany, thinking he wouldn't need it. Who would? Anyway, before we could mail a copy to him, he was already in the Army. We haven't heard from him since."

"Oh, how awful," sympathized Emma. "I know just what you're experiencing. My brother disappeared during the San Francisco earthquake in 1906. We've never learned what happened to him."

Jackie turned to Maddie, "It's going to be like looking for a needle in a haystack to find your brother."

"I know, but I've got to hope that somehow, with God's help, we'll be reunited."

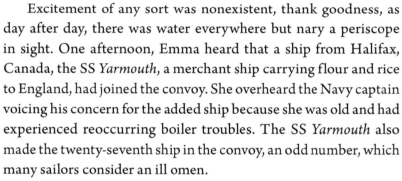

Excitement of any sort was nonexistent, thank goodness, as day after day, there was water everywhere but nary a periscope in sight. One afternoon, Emma heard that a ship from Halifax, Canada, the SS *Yarmouth*, a merchant ship carrying flour and rice to England, had joined the convoy. She overheard the Navy captain voicing his concern for the added ship because she was old and had experienced reoccurring boiler troubles. The SS *Yarmouth* also made the twenty-seventh ship in the convoy, an odd number, which many sailors consider an ill omen.

Even in 1917 sailors held with many superstitions, such as seeing rats fleeing a ship before it left port meant the vessel was doomed to sink. It was bad luck to set sail on Friday the 13th. Whistling while at sea was thought to challenge the weather and cause a severe storm. Many cooks always crushed eggshells before throwing them overboard, fearing half shells might be used by witches as boats to reach ships and cause havoc.

As days passed Emma, Jackie, and Maddie forgot about the added ship until one night they were roused from their sleep by the loudspeaker blasting, "All hands-on deck."

Emma slipped out of bed and got dressed. Jackie, Maddie, and Emma joined the Chief Nurse in the dining hall to see what was happening and if they might be needed. It wasn't long before they heard shuffling feet along the passageway and descending below. Looking out, they saw stretchers being carried down to where the ship's hospital was located. The Chief Nurse learned these were casualties from the explosion of the SS *Yarmouth*'s boiler.

Descending below, the nurses found the scene chaotic in the hospital area. Cots had been set up but not made. The injured lay sprawled on the floor. The doctor was nowhere in sight. Quickly, the Chief Nurse took charge; the cots were made and the patients placed on beds. Patients were cleaned up and the most seriously burned identified for treatment.

Emma had just retrieved her scissors from her pocket to cut the cloth from around a patient's burn when her arm was grabbed and her scissors forcibly taken. "No, you don't sister—I'm in charge here. Get your hands off my patient. You've no business here!" ordered a rum-smelling, shriveled-up unshaven gray-haired man wearing a torn T-shirt and brown stained denim trousers.

"Hold on there," ordered the Chief Nurse, striding over. "We're nurses, here to help."

"You can make beds and empty the bedpans but you're not to touch my patients. Get out NOW until I call for you."

Snatching her scissors from his hand, Emma followed the Chief Nurse as she signaled everyone to retreat.

"Did you see him rip the shirt off that burn victim as we left? He skinned the whole area!"

"He's no doctor—even the old-fashion barber would have had better sense."

"Now, ladies, let's not be too critical. Probably at one time he was the best they could hire," said the Chief Nurse.

4

Emma, Jackie, and Maddie sat looking at each other, thinking about the barbaric behavior of the ship's doctor they'd encountered. They waited the return of the Chief Nurse from her meeting with the naval Captain about their encounter with the doctor who obviously was prejudiced against nurses.

That wasn't anything new. In 1917, women still couldn't vote or own property, and many occupations were closed to them. A few women had ventured into the world of medicine but their credentials weren't accepted by all hospitals. Women were supposed to stay at home, take care of their men and children, and not have an opinion. In fact, only husbands were allowed to have one. Moreover, women were considered inferior to men intellectually. Recently, however, with the woman's suffrage movement supported by President Wilson, things were changing. There was a movement afoot to form a professional nursing organization in the United States like the Royal British Nurses' Association in England. Besides that, it looked very promising that a constitutional amendment could be passed in a couple of years granting women the right to vote.

Both Emma and Jackie smiled and nodded, squirming in their chairs in an effort to bring feeling back to their numb bottoms. Why was it taking the Chief Nurse so long?

Turning toward the door, Emma said, "Wish I was a fly on the wall where the Chief Nurse is reporting our encounter with the ships' doctor to the captain."

"Me too. I don't think she's one to mince words."

Smiling, Emma nodded. "I haven't been around her long, but her Tennessee background certainly comes out loud and clear in her language when her tentacles are up."

"*Neanderthal* was the nicest word she uttered in describing the doctor," grinned Jackie. "In polite company, I would have described him as obnoxious, stupid, and offensive. Why, he wouldn't even let any of us near the patients to cut off the cloth from around their burns."

"And to have grabbed my scissors like he did—it was bizarre!" exclaimed Emma.

"I resented his telling us we could make beds and empty the bedpans but nothing else," added Maddie tersely.

"When I told Wolfe I was going to nursing school," said Emma, "he warned me about the attitudes toward nurses. Some professionals at his medical school feel threatened by our profession, others don't."

"Could that be because decades ago people relied upon women herbalists?"

"Yes, perhaps. My great-grandmother knew how to treat ills with herbs. People called her 'Doctor O,'" remarked Maddie.

"Women who took on nursing duties during the Civil War were much appreciated. In some cases they acted as doctors. What happened between then and now that we've lost respect for our services and training?" asked Jackie looking around at the young nurses like herself who'd recently joined in waiting for the appearance of the Chief Nurse. "Will we ever be given the recognition we deserve?"

"Oh, I think we will," answered Emma. "We women are finally getting our backbone up to ask for the same rights as men. I think before we return home from this war, we'll be able a vote and have more of a say in our destiny."

"Do you really?"

"Yes," answered Emma as she heard the heavy clicking of heels entering the dining hall. Turning, she saw an erect, stern-faced Chief Nurse arrive.

All conversation ceased. "May I have your attention, ladies. I've consulted with Captain Willing about the situation with the ship's doctor. Under the current circumstances, we will not provide assistance to the ship's civilian doctor. An Army doctor is being transported from a nearby ship to ours to care for any and all patients during the remainder of the trip. As soon as he's aboard, we'll resume our duties and schedule as nurses." With that, she poured herself coffee and joined them at their table.

A buzz of conversation broke out amid nods. "Well, I guess that issue is settled," said Emma, turning toward Jackie and Maddie.

Winking at her companions, Jackie said, "I sure hope we get to stay under her command once we reach France. She's a real fighter."

Emma motioned agreement as they started walking toward the coffee urn being refilled by the ship's boy. As they moved between tables, even though they'd lengthened their stride, they found themselves bumping into tables. "Boy, are we going to have bruises with all this zigzagging!" complained Emma. "Thank goodness we should only have a little less than another week at sea. All this maneuvering to avoid the subs has added to our time onboard."

"We should count ourselves lucky we haven't been attacked," Maddie said.

Shaking their heads in agreement, Emma and Jackie took sips of coffee, lapsing deep in their own thoughts.

Emma took the opportunity to study her new friends. Jackie was the kind of person you'd like at your side in any emergency. Emma reminded herself that, since Jackie was a westerner like herself, she'd be stubbornly independent. Maddie's short blond hair matched her fair complexion, setting off an oval face with deep-set blue eyes accented by dark long eyelashes and eyebrows. Her nose wasn't sharp but slightly rounded at the tip, similar to most of Emma's relatives in Texas, including her papa. She appeared to be a very determined person, a goal setter, and very reliable. Emma looked forward to getting to know her better.

Since leaving New York City, all the women had dispensed with wearing makeup. They hadn't packed any, in fact, choosing to use the space for more important items like an extra sweater or notebook. And most of them looked forward to purchasing French makeup when they arrived in Paris. Wasn't it the most prized item among wealthy American women, especially the perfume?

Jackie's gaze returned to Emma. "I wonder if the others in our group are as anxious about what to expect when we get to France as we are."

Thinking before replying, Emma shifted in her seat. "Oh, I'm sure everyone is anxious. It's such an unknown. But few want to admit that they're a little fearful—I know I am. Some may already wish they hadn't volunteered. How about you?"

"Oh, I'm scared but I'm trying to see this as an adventure. Just think, we're going to be one of the first groups of American Army nurses to experience a world war, not just a civil war. What about you, Maddie?"

"I haven't given it much thought. I just want to get there and begin helping the British, French, and Belgian nurses who have been at this since 1914. Did you read about the group of nurses at an aid station in Belgium captured by the Germans? I heard they escaped with the help of their head sister."

Both Jackie and Emma shook their heads no. "Well, I hope we don't end up as prisoners. That would be scary," said Emma, shivering at the thought. "It's daunting enough wondering what we'll face daily, let alone in severe crises."

"Oh, Emma, you know what I mean. Have you wondered what kind of living quarters we'll have? Or what the hospitals will be like? The newspapers back home have only mentioned the horribly muddy conditions in the trenches," remarked Jackie, pulling her sweater sleeves down to cover her cold wrists.

"Yes, I know. We'll soon know what our troops will face once they're involved," said Emma. "I think it's ironic that President Wilson declared war on April 6th. It was in April 1906 that the great earthquake occurred in San Francisco."

"I hadn't realized that. How come you connected the dates?" asked Maddie.

"I was just a ten-year-old at the time, but I'll never forget the date," confided Emma. "My family was in San Francisco on vacation. For a time, I thought I'd lost both parents and brother."

"But I've heard you mention your parents?"

"Yes, my Mama's alive and the father I mentioned is a stepfather. My real papa died from injuries he got being trampled by horses."

"How awful for you! What about your brother?"

"We've never been able to trace him."

After a long pause, Jackie, in an effort to change the mood, said, "I read in the Denver paper before I left that our government is sending university history professors over to write about the war. Isn't that interesting?"

"Yes, but aren't our journalists in France doing that? Why historians?" Emma asked.

Jackie brushed her chin with one hand as if thinking before answering. "The newspaper article I read said the history professors are to write first-hand accounts of the history of the 'war to end all wars,' not the day-day-by actions taking place. If it's to be our last world war as the politicians say, a professionally written treatise on the subject is necessary."

"I don't believe that," answered Maddie, screwing up her face. "Men have been making war forever. This will not be the last great war fought. Think of Cain and Abel, our Civil War, and the Russian Civil War going on right now. Did you know that some American Red Cross nurses are going over to Russia to help?"

Before Jackie could reply, there was a rustle at the door and an Army officer entered along with Captain Willing. "Attention! May I have your attention! I wish to introduce the ship's replacement doctor that you all will be working under." Stepping aside and facing toward the young man standing to his left, he announced, "This is Lieutenant Leeds of the Army Medical Corps, who will be the ship's doctor until we reach England."

"Thank you. I understand you've already set up shifts to care for the wounded. I'll need the first group below as soon as possible. I look forward to working with you." The lieutenant nodded and left the mess area.

"Handsome guy, wouldn't you say," whispered Jackie following the doctor below to the hospital area.

"He's got silver bars on his collar. Is that a first lieutenant?" asked Emma.

"Yes, to both questions, but I like his tan, his black hair, and his chestnut eyes," whispered Maddie as she followed Emma.

"Well, I might be from Colorado, but this one is strikingly handsome with his chiseled features and sculptured sharp nose. Wonder if he's single? Did you see a ring?"

"Um, let's just hope he's not hung up on his own superiority as a physician," said Emma as they stepped off the last step.

The lower deck hall that served as the hospital overflow ward was dimly lit by a few overhead globes. The beds had been pushed up against the wall, leaving very little space for foot traffic. Down the hall, almost in the middle of the temporary ward, was the actual medical clinic.

Lieutenant Leeds side-stepped his way toward the clinic door, carefully avoiding patients' limbs hanging out into the passageway. Occasionally he stopped to check a moaning man or move a limb too far out to walk around.

5

Upon entering the temporary hospital ward, Emma and the other nurses followed the doctor. "Remove the bandages and clean the wounds so I can see what we've got. I'll be back. Come with me," he said, pointing to Jackie as he walked toward the clinic.

Emma stepped forward immediately and began following the doctor's orders as Jackie followed Lieutenant Leeds. It was heartbreaking to see how carelessly the men's clothing had been stripped from around the burn areas. Many nurse's eyes filled with tears. The duty hours slipped away as they treated the wounds, reapplied fresh bandages, and made the patients comfortable. Before Emma knew it, the second round of nurses arrived to relieve them.

As they climbed the stairs toward the dining hall, Jackie commented, "That was a pleasant change from our last session." A collective sigh answered the statement. Though drained and hungry, the nurses experienced the satisfaction of doing their job.

Emma said nothing, just smiled, as they entered the dining area, where they were greeted by tantalizing smells. Uniformed men and women sat at the tables. Seeing a long line waiting to pick up food, Emma groaned inwardly. Hurrying to get in the lunch line, she swallowed and ran her tongue around her mouth. She hadn't picked up sufficient food at breakfast to sustain her, a self-imposed transgression since joining the Army and facing buffet lines at meals. Sight of all the food displayed tended to ruin her appetite despite a protesting stomach.

Finally reaching the neatly stacked trays, she quickly looked down the line at what foods were offered. Taking a deep whiff, she smiled, a twinkle in her eye, and turned to Jackie. "Ah, our favorite, minced beef gravy on toast!"

"Joy of joys," whispered Jackie with a wink. "What's with pouring gravy over everything?"

"Hides what's really on top of the toast. What do you think? We're lucky—no need to worry about dieting," whispered Emma.

"You should talk—you're already skin and bones."

"No, I'm not," came Emma's retort, beckoning to the person behind the serving table for a spoonful of minced beef over the cold crispy toast. "You're the skinny one."

"Could you two move it along?" came a gruff voice behind them. "Some of us peons want to eat before nightfall."

Emma quickly slid her tray forward, ignoring the person who'd complained, but when she reached for an orange, she snuck a look at the very tall and handsome sailor behind them. Nudging Jackie, she indicated with her eyes to take a look. *That is one gorgeous hunk of a man*, she thought.

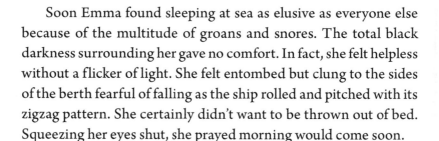

Soon Emma found sleeping at sea as elusive as everyone else because of the multitude of groans and snores. The total black darkness surrounding her gave no comfort. In fact, she felt helpless without a flicker of light. She felt entombed but clung to the sides of the berth fearful of falling as the ship rolled and pitched with its zigzag pattern. She certainly didn't want to be thrown out of bed. Squeezing her eyes shut, she prayed morning would come soon.

With the Army doctor, the nurses helped with sick call like on every Army post. It was first thing in the morning and because Emma was assigned the early morning duty, she found herself half fumbling, bleary eyed, through the breakfast line before descending to the hospital. She noticed that no matter how groggy she was upon presenting herself for duty, Dr. Leeds greeted her with a smile and a hardy "Good morning!" *How could he be so energetic so early in the morning*, she wondered.

Emma found dealing with the flood of men reporting in with all sorts of common ailments such as colds, sore throats, sprains, and minor cuts rewarding. The more serious cases were passed on to the doctor. Emma loved the work, even if some came on the pretense of being ill to receive attention. She'd put on her sisterly hat, thinking how she would want her brother to be treated in a similar situation. She talked to them about home or interests while taking their temperature and checking their blood pressure before sending them back to duty, hopefully in a better frame of mind.

She'd never worked in an emergency for any length of time and never in a doctor's office before the shipboard duty. She discovered she enjoyed the freedom of solving minor medical ailments without the supervision of a doctor. Back in Santa Fe, she'd found working in surgery rewarding because it drastically improved the patients' lives. And she expected that most of her time in France she'd do the same, considering the majority of war causalities would require surgery.

During off-duty time, Emma noticed that there were clusters of nurses playing bridge, something she had never taken any interest in, and a few sat knitting and chatting. She wished she'd thought of bringing her knitting. It would have kept her fingers nimble for the time she could once again play her violin. Too bad she didn't have room for her instrument. She heard that one soldier on board had managed to bring his ukulele with him. Lucky him! She wondered how he'd managed to conceal it to bring it along.

On those rare occasions when they were allowed to walk the ship's deck to get some fresh air, Emma heard music in the waves as the ship cut through the water. Looking over the railing, she visualized nymphs playing sonatas urging the ship on its dancing course. Of course, she never divulged her musings to others—they would have thought her crazy and probably sent her packing. No, she never said a word, not even to Jackie or Maddie, who'd become her closest friends.

Emma wrote letters during some of her free time, especially to Wolfe and her mama. Of course, no mail was received or sent while they were at sea. The ship had wireless contact with the other ships in the convoy, although she noticed that they seemed to communicate more with flag signals. Perhaps that was so the subs couldn't intercept the messages as easily as they could the wireless.

She looked forward to a large packet of letters upon her arrival in England or France. She missed knowing about her Mama's health. Her stepfather, Jamie, in his last letter mentioned Mama had been having bouts of memory loss. None of the doctors in Santa Fe could give him an explanation for it but had suggested that perhaps she needed to cut down on the number of piano students she taught. Jamie wrote that he'd hired a housekeeper to relieve the stress of housework but also to have someone to keep an eye on Mama.

Emma wondered how the draft was going in New Mexico since the government declared that Native Americans could be drafted. At first, they hadn't been considered citizens of the United States, so they were excluded from joining any of the armed forces. But soon, draft boards in the Southwest began to push for their inclusion. The government ruled that local draft boards could decide for themselves who was a citizen and who wasn't. Emma was pleased that many of her Native American friends, eager to serve, were allowed to volunteer.

The letters that Emma looked forward to the most of course would be those from Wolfe, her fiancé, who had preceded her to Europe in an advance group of physicians to plan for the influx of medical personnel and set up American hospital facilities. She hadn't heard from him since his departure from New York City, but they had tentatively agreed to meet in Paris when she arrived.

Juan, her childhood friend with the Army's Veterinary Service, where his degree in veterinary science would make use of his talents, first though he'd end up serving in Italy where the majority of the horses and mules were shipped. In the end, his orders sent him to France. Emma expected a large packet of letters from him waiting for her when she arrived in France.

Emma was amazed that all three of them, Wolfe, Juan, and herself, would be in Europe, hopefully France. How was that for serendipity! *Did God have a plan up his sleeve?* she wondered. Her faith had taught her that nothing happened in a vacuum. As when she was a child, she again saw God sitting up among the fluffy clouds at his chess board smiling to himself while he moved around the chess pieces, representing people. In Emma's vision, the person playing with God sat covered in thick mist. Was his name Free Will?

6

After Maddie finished her shift at the hospital, she joined Jackie and Emma in the dining hall for a cup of coffee and a cookie, if there were any left. Whereas both Jackie and Emma had attended nursing schools operated by Catholic sisters, Maddie graduated from a state school begun as the John Sealy Hospital Training School for Nurses, the oldest school in the Southwest, established in 1890. For years, it was managed by a board of lady managers as an independent institution, but in 1896 it became the first nursing school in the state to be affiliated with the University of Texas. Maddie touted that she was one of twenty-six graduating nurses of 1916, large by any standard for a nursing school. Upon graduation, she'd joined the Red Cross first, not knowing about the Army Nurse Corps until later, when most of the Red Cross nurses transferred into the Army Nurse Corps as reservists. Because Emma never joined the Red Cross, her status in the Corps was as a regular Army nurse, which gave her the privilege of remaining in the Army until retirement age. If she'd been a reservist, that wouldn't have been possible.

"Emma, are you going to take the Chief Nurse's exam when we reach France? I hear the Army is in need of applicants."

Looking at Maddie, Emma replied, "No, I don't feel qualified yet. Maybe after a few months of battlefield experience, I'll feel ready."

"I'm with you on not feeling qualified, "said Jackie. "I wouldn't have felt ready to tangle with the situation we faced onboard ship here."

"I'm a neophyte, as far as the Army's concerned." Allie drawled. "I'm here to serve and hopefully find a husband."

Emma glanced at her fellow Texan, startled that she confessed to seeking a helpmate. That would be the last public pronouncement she'd consider voicing. It was too personal. Looking around the group, she couldn't help but wonder how many others secretly hoped to connect with a mate.

Sometimes when Emma walked, she was so lost in thought that she failed to notice activity occurring around her, as happened as they neared the coast of Ireland. Dimly, she heard the siren sound, then the rush of men surging past. Pushed to the side, she watched as lifeboats were lowered. Squinting in the direction they rowed, she noticed a funnel of smoke. As she watched, she felt a sudden cramp hit her stomach. The German subs were at it again! Sinking everything they could. Some of their convoy had just changed course that morning, heading for Ireland rather than Liverpool because they needed fuel.

"All hands on deck to receive survivors," blasted from the ship's speaker.

Emma found herself among the silent watchers as the lifeboats began to return. Intent upon the action, she didn't notice Allie, another nurse who'd taken to disliking her, sidle up behind her. "Those Krauts should be wiped off the face of the earth. Even the American ones!"

Shaken, Emma turned from the railing, bumping into a scowling Captain Andrews speaking to Allie. "Talk like that has no place here. Leave the deck."

During supper that night, the dining hall was unusually quiet. Metal trays were carefully placed on the tables, conversation was hushed, and no complaints about the food was heard. Emma sat with Jackie and Maddie, silently scooping up every gravy-covered morsel of corned beef and toast. Thoughts spun around in her head. She was alive but somewhere out there in the deep blue sea, many young men her age had died because the ship they'd been on had been sunk. What had been their last thoughts as they met death? Why did so many die? What if it had been their ship that sunk? Shaking her head, Emma stood up and bussed her tray, silently thanking God she was alive.

Following Jackie, Emma descended and sought her berth. Turning to her friend, Emma asked, "Are you as shaken as I am?"

"Yes, but life goes on. We go on living," answered Jackie swaying with the zigzag movement. Straightening up upon hearing voices coming toward them, she motioned for Emma to step aside to let others past.

"Tomorrow's going to be rough."

"I know—all eyes will be watchful. I hear they've doubled the alert to not throw anything overboard; it alerts the subs where we are."

"Thank goodness we're sailing into Brest, France, after the arrival of our fleet of yachts," commented Jackie. "They've been so swift and maneuver so rapidly, the German subs hardly had a chance. Those yachtsmen who volunteered to come over are real heroes, I say."

"I never thought much of the rich and their privileged pastimes but my respect for them has changed. They've created naval history for America, I hear," ventured Emma.

"Their gunners are super too, I hear."

"Thank goodness …"

Emma touched Jackie's arm, urging her to follow her toward the showers. She'd heard enough about war, no need to hear more to worry about all night. She was worried enough about making it into Liverpool and on to France.

7

The nurses scurried around the next morning packing their belongings and making certain they had all their identification. The night before, during supper, they'd learned that the women would be the last group departing the ship, as the soldiers would disembark first.

Like all the nurses, Emma anticipated stepping onto firm English soil. She was tired of being confined to a "rolling tin can," as she laughingly referred to the ship. She missed the wide-open spaces of New Mexico, the rugged bluish-purple mountains that made her feel secure, and the clear blue cloudless sky above. Glancing around the group of nurses, she suddenly realized how colorless everyone appeared, including herself, with their pale faces and brownish uniforms, all speaking American with different accents. She hoped she wouldn't have any trouble with British English. How she missed hearing the mixture of Spanish, Mexican, and Navajo spoken at home.

The main topic of conversation as they waited to disembark involved whether they'd go directly to London and then on to France. Would there be time for sightseeing? Would they still have an indoctrination by the British sisters as they'd been told before leaving home?

Most of the merchant ships in their convoy had been diverted to Irish ports for refueling or around to the North Sea to the port at Aberdeen, Scotland, where there was plenty of coal. Only the troop ships headed into Liverpool.

"Okay, ladies, they're ready for us to disembark. We'll be going through customs, so be ready to show your Army identification," said the Chief Nurse. Each nurse carefully walked down the rough gangway, holding on to the railing on the right side. Emma found herself a little tipsy at first as she stepped onto firm ground.

Again, as when they left New York, the nurses stood in a slow-moving line, while the officials checked their cards. Once they were assembled on the dock, a British officer read them a welcoming message from King George V. Afterward, they marched to the local station to board the train to Southampton. For the first time, they were together as nurses with no other female service personnel. After chatting excitedly about their arrival in England, they settled down to watch the green fields surrounded by hedge rows. Emma longingly watched for sheep, recalling the herds grazing on the sparse desert of New Mexico. *These pampered English sheep don't have to work very hard for a mouthful of grass*, she thought.

Their accommodations that night was on an ambulance ship, where beds were made up for them in the former dining hall. The meal that night was served to them on their beds.

"I've heard of breakfast in bed," commented the Chief Nurse, "but this is my first dinner in bed." That brought the first burst of uproarious laughter from the entire group since arriving.

The overnight voyage across the English Channel must have been calm and uneventful because Emma slept soundly in her lower berth, awaking in the same position in the morning that she'd fallen into bed in the night before. Their ship lay in the harbor in Brest, France, waiting its turn at docking. Brest, one of two important shipping entry points used by the British, teemed with transport ships arriving from England. Soon it would welcome troop ships arriving from America, just like theirs.

"They're ready for us to disembark," announced the Chief Nurse. "Let's line up and have your identification in hand."

Looking around as she waited her turn, Emma spied a crumbling stone fortress at the water's edge. She could envision it being magnificent in times past. What had been its purpose—guarding the harbor from invaders? Soon she found herself at the front of the line showing her identification, allowing the official to search through her duffle, and answering questions. Once through, they waited until everyone was cleared and then started walking to the nunnery where they'd be billeted while receiving training by the British Expeditionary Force nurses before being given their assignments.

As she became more confident in walking on solid ground, Emma couldn't help noticing how many shops were boarded up. Other than their group, few people were on the streets and those they did pass stared vacantly at them. After a few blocks, they came upon women standing in a line waiting to get into the bakery. Strangely, the women weren't talking to each other. Back home, women always chatted, sharing news and gossiping. Looking at the faces in the line, Emma saw vacant, gaunt masks. Their clothing was worn but clean. The heels of shoes appeared scruffy and in some cases were tied on with strips of old fabric. A few children stood listlessly by their mothers in mismatched clothing and oversized sweaters.

Emma's eyes smarted as she thought, *So, this is what three years of war looks like ... desperation and hunger.* The newspapers back home had reported that the French and British forces were near defeat and that all hope of victory lay in the entry of the United States into the war. As she continued up the street, she began to notice the absence of males, young or old. Did this mean they'd all gone to the war?

Finally, they stopped in front of a three-story hewn-stone structure next to a building with a steeple. "Ladies, we have arrived," said the Chief Nurse as she approached the small door of the building and knocked. After a brief wait, it was opened by a black-habited nun who took one look at the Chief Nurse and those behind her and beckoned all to enter.

Silently, they were led through a maze of halls to a large room housing rows of beds along each side of the room. The nun bowed to the Chief Nurse and left. "Well, ladies," she said, glancing around, "Guess this is ours, so choose a bed and settle in."

The room was dimly light by bare light bulbs hanging from the high ceiling above. The whitewashed walls, yellowish with age, showed a few waist-high black marks, probably caused by the metal bed railings. Lined up along one wall close to the ceiling, twelve tiny windows winked down through brownish streaks. The single metal beds were freshly made with clean sheets, one small pillow, and a gray blanket. It looked like heaven to Emma. No more climbing up into a bunk.

"Ladies, let me introduce you to Sister Agatha, who is with the British Expeditionary Force and is in charge of our training," announced the Chief Nurse, who stood by a tall upright woman wearing a blue cape draped over one shoulder beneath a starched white dress falling just above sturdy oxfords.

Sister Agatha glanced around at the young women standing beside the beds in the room before beginning to speak. "Welcome to Brest, ladies. We are so happy to have you assist us in caring for our wounded. If you will follow me, I will take you to the hospital where your training will be held." Turning, she walked back through the nunnery hall and out to the street. Having not been walking for several weeks except around a ship's deck, Emma felt like she was running to keep up, as did most of the other nurses. The cobblestone streets were uneven and unfamiliar, causing a few missteps and expletives from many.

"Gotta kept one eye on the ground or we'll sprain an ankle," muttered the person next to Emma.

Seated in a dining hall that had once been elegant but was now shabby, the nurses sipped mugs of hot tea and nibbled on biscuits, wishing for an Epsom salts bath for their aching feet. Jackie smiled as she raised her mug to Emma. "Cheerio!"

Lightly tapping Jackie's mug, Emma said, "Likewise!"

For the rest of the afternoon, the nurses, divided into groups, toured the hotels now turned into hospitals. They learned that Brest was the shipping point for most of the English patients headed home for further medical treatment. In other words, the ones who probably would never return to the trenches on French soil but would battle a personal conflict as a result of their injuries. So now they understood why they'd traveled across the English Channel in an empty hospital ship.

After supper, the fatigued nurses returned to the nunnery for their first night on French soil. Emma, lying in a well-worn crevice in the middle of her mattress, replayed in her mind all that she'd seen on their tour. Many of the patients lay listlessly, not even aware of people passing. Some reached out, seeming to beg for physical contact or just acknowledgement. There were soldiers without limbs or sightless. Smiles were few and laughter scarce.

Emma thought back on the pain she'd experienced during the weeks her papa had lain nonresponsive in a coma before his death. She wondered if she'd grown thick skinned enough to sustain her working with war-wounded patients.

Assigned to the furthest hospital from her lodging, Emma found herself along with Pinkie, from New York City, trudging up the slightly inclining street called Rue de Siam, the main street in Brest, headed toward the Penfeld River and a swinging bridge. Their raincoats billowed out in the wind blowing down the street. Their wide-brimmed hats had to be held onto against playful gusts. Making their way even harder was the stream of lorries and ambulances headed in the opposite direction toward the harbor. One morning as they battled the wind, rain, and traffic, an ambulance stopped close beside them and a head stuck out the door. "You gals like a ride up to the hospital?"

Clutching their hats, both Emma and Pinkie yelled, "Yes!" And giving a smile, they scrambled into the vehicle.

"Thought you might," said the driver. "My chum and I noticed you on our way down to the harbor. Devil of a rain and wind today."

"We thank you for the ride," said Emma. "I never thought France would be so cold and rainy, especially near the west coast."

"That's Brest for you. Where you girls from?" inquired the second British soldier, sitting on the right side of Pinkie.

"We're from the States."

"Wow! You got into this mess over here. I just heard that your President Wilson declared war on Germany. Welcome to the brawl."

"Thank you, I think. We're one of the first groups to arrive. We've only been here a couple of days," shared Pinkie, glancing at the sandy-haired young man beside her. "You must work at the hospital where we're training."

"Right ho!" answered the driver. "We're ferrying the lucky ones down to the harbor. Their fighting days are over."

Emma turned to the speaker. "Sounds like you'd like to be going home too. How long have you been over here?"

"I've been here since '14, shot up, and reassigned to the ambulance service. Never been home. I miss—woops, we're here."

Entering the hospital, Emma and Pinkie found themselves in a crowded hallway with stretchers, wheelchairs, and happy-faced men on crutches or leaning on canes, all waiting for transportation to the dock. Smiling broadly, the two made their way through the group, stopping here and there, shaking hands and saying, "Good luck!"

A very pleased matron greeted them near the end of the hall. "Seems you two have the right personality for this job. Come and have a cuppa tea to warm your bones. The rain is like ice this morning."

Emma spent the morning assigned to a ward of newly arrived patients who required fresh dressings and medications. Some lay silently as she worked at making them comfortable but many asked, "Do you know when I'll be going home?" They knew what being in Brest meant.

"Keep watching for infection," reminded the ward sister. "Just because they've made it this far doesn't mean they're out of the woods yet." Over and over, the medical staff reminded the nurses about the battlefield conditions that work against a patient: mud, bacteria, and deplorable circumstances in the trenches.

What did the surgeon lecture us on? thought Emma. The wound was just the entry point inviting all the bacteria from the trenches, the person's own slimy, mud-caked clothing; the contact with others as they were moved to an aid station, the lorry transporting the patient … everywhere bacteria crept in to attack.

As Emma listened to the lecturing physician, she thought of how simple a gunshot wound had been back home compared to a battlefield. No worrying about the environment, only the entry site of the wound. Here as a nurse, she was just as much as a soldier battling a secretive Army attacking the body as the soldiers in the trenches. She visualized them as evil-faced invaders, body snatchers of the worst kind.

"Good evening!" greeted the nurses as they settled at the end of the hall where they were billeted. The Chief Nurse looked around at her "wonderful sisters," as she called them, before speaking, "Thank you all for arranging to be back from your respective hospital assignments and suppers. I have news for you. Tomorrow, most of you will be headed out to your assigned stations …" Clapping interrupted as the nurses turned to each other, smiling. "Some of you will be assigned to aid stations close to the front, others to advanced dressing stations further away from the fighting, and a few of you to hospitals located in safe areas." Silence greeted this last announcement. "In the next few days, I will be posting your assignments along with the day you'll leave. Most of you will be transported by motorized ambulance. Tomorrow you have a day off to explore the town." With that pronouncement, she stepped aside to answer individual questions.

Emma looked around for Jackie and made her way toward her. "Thank goodness our orientation is over. I'm ready to face the frightening world out there. Want to do something tomorrow?"

Jackie nodded, "Let's explore. Maybe walk the beach."

"That sounds fun. Perhaps we can pick up something at the bakery for a picnic before heading for the beach."

"Hey, Emma," yelled Pinkie, rushing up. "I heard we were going to have the day off so I rented a horse and cart. How about a drive into the countryside with me tomorrow?"

8

Dear Wolfe,

Wouldn't you know it, we were given the day off before leaving Brest for our duty stations and both Pinkie and Jackie came down with influenza. We'd planned to go to the beach and have a picnic but so goes the best laid plans! Here I am, at the nunnery, serving as nurse to both my friends and making use of my time by writing letters. I did walk down to the bakery mid-morning to purchase a couple of croissants and a pot of loganberry jam so I'd have something to eat instead of thin vegetable soup with the silent Sisters of Mary Magdalene. It's not that they haven't fed us well, but their rule of silence is difficult to follow. You know how I love to chat.

By this afternoon, more of the nurses had returned to quarters feeling sick. Will any of us be able to travel tomorrow? The Chief Nurse hasn't returned yet. So she's unaware we may be facing an epidemic.

I finished my surgical orientation two days ago. Have you seen The Guidebook on Surgical Nursing in War by Elizabeth Bundy? Or did you get a similar book for doctors when you arrived? It was interesting that at least the nurses' book started out explaining how to comfort the patient, for instance, types of pillows and where to place them to ease pain; how to use newspaper under a patient to keep him warm, something I never would have thought of coming from the southwest! Then, the guide went into the different kinds of microbodies picked up on the battlefield that infect and impede recovery. That part of the manual I found very interesting.

I have asked for a surgical assignment but haven't heard whether it will be granted. So I can't tell you where I'll be. Since I haven't received a letter from you since leaving home, I don't know where you are. I've asked every doctor I've met here if they've heard of you with no success, but I haven't given up hope. The nursing sisters tell me that it takes time to start receiving mail but eventually letters do get through. I do miss you, especially not knowing exactly where you are. I worry. On the ship coming over, all I dreamed about was meeting you in Paris. Yes, I know I'm a romantic and the capital of France fed into my dreams. I wanted to walk hand in hand with you, experience dining at an outdoor café, enjoying a glass of wine, kiss you in the middle of a bridge, and oh so many other things. Please write and tell me that we'll get to do it all before going back home

Stay safe, my love,
Emma

"Emma, we've got our assignments. They've just been posted," shouted Jackie, rushing into their dormitory at the nunnery. "Both of us leave soon by train for a casualty clearing station in the east. Hurry—we have to be at the train depot in an hour."

As her fellow nurses began packing their gear, Emma returned to her own bed and hurriedly began gathering her belongings. The once overstuffed bag was now bulging with newly government-issued necessities like a proper pair of galoshes, a gas mask, and a hard helmet for air raids. Holding up her metal hat and gas mask, Emma asked, "Jackie, where are you packing these?"

Stopping midstream in her packing, Jackie turned toward Emma. "Oh, except for the galoshes that I'll wear, I'm hanging them on the outside of my bag."

Grinning, Emma nodded to her friend. "That's sensible."

Trekking along in her oversized footwear through puddles of water and mud carrying ungainly baggage, Emma, along with several other nurses, entered the Brest train depot. Pushing their way through the crowd using their duffle bags like battering rams, they soon found the numbered pole they'd been instructed to wait near. "Look at all the people waiting for the same train we are!" Jackie murmured placing her bag between her feet for safety.

Lowering her bag to the floor, Emma brought one foot up on it to rub a cramp. "I hope we don't have to stand all the way to our destination." She rubbed up and down on the painful spot of her leg until the pain eased. Standing up straight, she glanced around and detected earthy woolen odors so common in crowded places in New Mexico. Inhaling the familiar smell, Emma's tension eased, and a smile crept across her face.

As the train pulled into the station and stopped, Emma watched the people separate, allowing passengers to exit. "Attention au depart," came a command. Emma was shoved forward toward the train, her bag pushed against her legs just below her knees. Her helmet cut into her leg, causing a quick intake of breath. "Emma, save me a seat," shouted Jackie, who'd become separated from her.

Reaching the car steps, Emma tried lifting her bag up but, pushed from behind, she couldn't get enough of a grip to heave it up. Gritting her teeth, she tugged harder just as she felt a hand reach around and ease the bag up the step. Before she could say "thank you" she felt herself being lifted up into the compartment. Steadying herself, she shoved her bag toward a seat close to the inside door. "There's plenty of seats," said the man who'd helped her board. "You don't need to sit way over there. Take a window seat."

"Thank you," mumbled Emma, glancing at the gentleman wearing a heavy Irish knit sweater, who spoke with an American accent. "I was scared I was going to be crushed in that crowd. You saved me."

"Glad to be of service, ma'am."

"Woo, there you are," said Jackie, breathlessly plunking herself and her bag down beside Emma. "I thought I'd be crushed by that crowd."

Soon the compartment filled up. People kept looking in for seats and uttering angry expressions as they turned away. Emma and Jackie sat shoulders together near the window away from the inside door. Then they heard another "Attention au depart" and the sound of doors slamming and felt the movement of the train. They were on their way east, to the war's front.

9

Almost immediately, Jackie started chatting with the two men sitting across from them. Shy and retiring, Emma wanted to enter into the conversation but found herself thinking about what to say, unsure of how to articulate her thoughts to strangers. Discouraged with herself, she turned to look out the window. For a while, they traveled close enough that she glimpsed water through the rain and fog as the train chugged along, climbing a slight incline out of Brest. As time passed, they broke out into lovely green fields with rolling hills in the distance. As the train picked up speed, she tuned back into the conversation of her seatmates and heard Jackie making tentative plans with the two men to see a little of Paris with them.

"Will we have time for sightseeing?" Emma intervened.

Jackie nodded. "Want to join us for a short tour? We'll only have about two hours before we must join the convoy taking us to our final destination."

Emma straightened up. "Two whole hours? I wonder if I could find out about Wolfe's whereabouts?"

The man who'd helped Emma onto the train asked, "Who's Wolfe?"

"He's her fiancé, an Army doctor," interrupted Jackie before Emma could reply.

"Oh, is he stationed in Paris?"

Brushing her hand across Jackie's hip, Emma answered, "I don't know where he's at for sure, since I haven't heard from him since he arrived in France, but I think he's in Paris."

Watching, Emma heard one say to the other, "It shouldn't be too difficult to locate him if he's in Paris."

Emma looked askance at the two. *How could they find out?* she wandered. Turning to Jackie she whispered, "How can they do something I haven't got any idea how to do?"

"Well, if you'd been listening to our conversation, you'd have heard that they work at the American embassy."

"Oh my, I did miss a lot!"

Tom and Bob ignored the whisperings going on across from them. Embarrassed, Emma cocked her head first one way and then the other before asking, "Have you both just arrived in France?"

"No," answered the one who'd helped Emma onto the train. "Tom and I have been stationed at the embassy since 1916."

Pausing, Emma asked, "It must have been exciting to be here a year before we entered the war."

"Well, I wouldn't call it exciting, exactly. Unnerving, yes."

"Why do you say that?" asked Jackie.

"Well, the Germans advanced quickly as the outnumbered French kept retreating. You did know that the Germans almost took Paris, didn't you?"

"Yes," answered Emma, "But I didn't realize it was that bad. Being from New Mexico, I'd paid closer attention to Mexico's invasion of our state."

Nodding, the man, whose name was Tom, clutched his knees as if experiencing the fear of the German's invasion again. "Yes, I read about that. Supposedly, the German government encouraged the Mexicans to pick a fight with us hoping it would keep us from entering the war against them."

"Thank goodness it didn't work," muttered Bob.

Silence ensued between the four passengers as they thought about their discussion of the war. Emma recalled Juan's injury when Columbus, New Mexico, was raided by Pancho Villa. Her friend had been lucky to survive the surprise attack. Then, General Pershing and his contingent of soldiers were ordered to run the Mexicans back into their own country. Thank goodness President Wilson hadn't declared war but just ordered federal troops down to the boarder.

For a moment, all discussion ceased as all considered what could've or would've happened if the president hadn't made that particular decision. Looking out the window, Emma observed the low-hanging clouds over the landscape, giving the fields an eerie, unnatural look. *Do the French believe in leprechauns like the Irish?* she wondered. If she'd been raised in France, she could easily have believed in the existence of "little people" scampering among the green fields and hills, teasing folks with their antics. How different the French countryside was compared to the English with its hedgerows dividing the fields. The French used fences like in America.

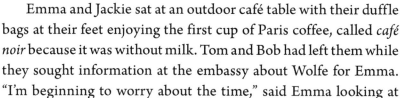

Emma and Jackie sat at an outdoor café table with their duffle bags at their feet enjoying the first cup of Paris coffee, called *café noir* because it was without milk. Tom and Bob had left them while they sought information at the embassy about Wolfe for Emma. "I'm beginning to worry about the time," said Emma looking at her watch. Thirty minutes had already lapsed of their two-hour travel break.

"Patience—they'll come through for us, I just know it," said Jackie, sitting down her cup. "Can you believe we're sitting at an outdoor café in Paris?! Wait until I write my mom—she'll wet her pants!"

Smiling broadly at her friend's exuberance, Emma bobbed her head. "Yes, my mom would too, except she's too reserved to show any reaction."

Suddenly, the two men appeared and stood shoulder to shoulder in front of them looking woebegone. Emma's heart sank as she surveyed their soberness. She braced herself for the news that Wolfe wasn't in Paris.

"Ta-da!" sang out Tom and Bob as they parted, revealing Wolfe.

Emma leaped up and threw herself into his arms and the two became indistinguishable. Onlookers clapped as they watched the loving pair embrace in the city of romance. Whispering in her ear, Wolfe said, "I've hired a carriage, so we can be alone until you have to leave. Come." Picking up Emma's duffle bag, he guided her toward a waiting carriage.

"We'll meet you at the depot with Jackie," shouted Tom, throwing Jackie's bag in with Emma's. Chuckling, the three newly minted musketeers walked off arm in arm to explore the city.

10

Emma put her arm through Wolfe's and cuddled up, shoulder to shoulder, nuzzling him and breathing in his clean masculine scent as he guided the gig. She was rewarded by a throaty groan.

Wolfe turned toward her, his deep blue eyes sparkling, and spoke to her before turning back to the tangled Paris traffic encircling them. "You look so beautiful, my love. It's been too long. I've missed you more than I care to admit." Moving the reins to his left hand, he slid the other around her waist to pull her almost onto his lap.

Emma felt a flutter in her stomach that engulfed her. She'd never experienced such a strong reaction before, and the thrill of it tugged at her heart. Grasping the surrounding hand, she gave it a squeeze. She felt warm lips touch her cheek as she raised up and responded with a kiss to his. Content sitting quietly together, her heart beat to the clip-clop of the horse's hooves on the street, her gaze on the profile of her love beside her.

"Shall we walk?" asked Wolfe, bringing the horse to a stop at the side of a river walk area.

Jostled from her serenity, Emma faintly murmured, "Oh, yes. Let's!"

Tying the reins to a figureheaded post, Wolfe helped Emma down from the buggy. "I've dreamed of us walking along this river ever since arriving in Paris," he said guiding her hand to his bent arm. "I've watched couples ambling along here and wished I had you with me." Bending close, he gave Emma a full kiss on her lips.

Smothering her delight, Emma moved closer to him. "This is more romantic than doing the river walk in San Antonio, don't you think?"

"You bet."

"How long do you think you'll be stationed in Paris?" asked Emma.

Slowing his pace, he clasped her hand in his and squeezed. "I have no idea how long I'll be here. The fighting isn't going well, casualties are mounting, and the need for doctors at the British Regimental aid posts is crucial. I've volunteered but don't know how soon I'll be sent. What about you? Do you know where you're going?"

"Not exactly. All twenty of us are supposedly being sent to casualty clearing station 12, but where that is I don't know."

"Mmm, we might end up close enough together that we can visit occasionally. If we are, we can travel back and forth with one of the ambulances."

"We'll hope," murmured Emma falling silent beside Wolfe.

"Have you heard from Santa Fe? I haven't gotten any letters, even from you."

"I'm not surprised. Although the mail service is pretty good here, it does take time. Receiving letters from the States takes weeks because priority is given to troops and supplies. Food is really scarce because the German subs and U-boats have been so successful at sinking the supply ships from England. I received a letter last week from my paw. You knew he sold the farm in Texas and moved back as your stepfather's buyer, didn't you?"

"No, I hadn't heard. Why did he sell out?" asked Emma.

Brushing his hand through his hair, Wolfe replied, "Said the farm held too many memories of Mom and thoughts of the hired man she ran away with to Mexico. But anyway, he's happy back in

Santa Fe and traveling, mostly up to Denver and Boise, buying and selling."

"No more trips to Mexico?" asked Emma.

"No," answered Wolfe swinging her around so they faced each other.

"Did he happen to mention how Mama and Jamie are doing?"

"Both seem to be happy as larks. Your mom has more music students than she can handle and Jamie has invested in Fritz's cattle and sheep business. With the war, the demand for meat has doubled."

"Well, I guess they're not missing us much," said Emma swinging away from Wolfe. "Beat you to the fountain over there," challenged Emma, legs flying.

"Oh no you don't," hooted Wolfe, sprinting after his fleeing sweetheart. Within minutes, she looked back to see him within arm's reach. She squealed. Pinned by his arms and covered by his body, she went limp and felt the thrill of his love seep into her.

"You promise you'll be careful at the front?" she whispered.

"I won't be right at the front, dearest. Don't worry, I'm coming back to you."

"You better or I'll come up to heaven and haunt you to the end of time."

Chuckling, "And I just bet you'd do that. There'd be no peace anywhere, even if I ended up in hell." Stroking the loose strands of hair from her face, he added, "But that's not going to happen. You don't have to worry about my getting killed. If I made it following you through all your childish adventures in Texas, you're not going to get rid of me easily."

"That's just it, I want you safe. Why didn't you volunteer for a general hospital where I'd know you'd be safe?"

"Why didn't you ask for an assignment at a general hospital where your talent as a surgical nurse could be used?" Emma felt his arms tighten around her, cradling her head on his shoulder and his thigh muscles straddle her legs. Lying there on the soft green turf felt glorious; a lifetime of nights would be heavenly.

Suddenly, the moment was gone as Wolfe helped her stand. "I think I better get you back." Taking her hand, he began leading her in the direction buggy.

Struggling to overcome the many sensations she'd experienced, Emma was thankful for Wolfe's supporting hand, since her shoes weren't cooperating with her feet. Finally reaching where they'd left the horse, Wolfe stopped and gazed at her. With a rakish smile, he said, "I think you'd better straighten your uniform."

Embarrassed, Emma looked down at the leaves and grass clinging to her skirt. Her uniform jacket buttons were undone, the jacket disheveled. Wide eyed, Emma looked up at Wolfe. "Oh, what should I do? I can't report looking like this."

Laughing, Wolfe shook his head.

"Don't you dare laugh at me," said Emma, slapping him.

"Come on, I'll take you to my place and Jerry, my right-hand man, will fix you up."

"Do we have time?" Emma asked as he helped her into the buggy.

"We'll hurry. Don't worry—schedules are always late in Paris. We have plenty of time."

11

Arriving at their duty station, the nurses walked through mud several inches deep past rain-drenched tents until finally stopping in front of the one that would be theirs. Stepping inside, Emma saw two rows of six cots mounded with bedding and pillows. "Find a bed and get settled in. I'll be back in fifteen minutes to take you for a tour of the hospital." With that, the sister who'd met them on their arrival left.

Emma waited patiently to choose a cot while those around her made their choices. Mentally dazed from having to leave Wolfe so soon and then travel in a cramped ambulance for hours to the duty station, she felt sluggish. After making her bed, she slid her duffle bag between her cot and the one next to hers, creating a makeshift night stand. Tired, she started to sit down but, glancing around, noticed most everyone headed for the door. Sighing and looking longingly at her bed, she followed.

The rain pelted them as they slogged slowly through the mud toward a miserable-looking schoolhouse. Upon entering the main hallway, the sister whispered softly, "Please remove your rubbers but keep your coats on. There's very little heat."

Shivering, Emma slipped off her mud-caked galoshes, wondering how she'd be able to identify hers later since all six pairs were alike. "Hope we're all wearing the same size, large, so there won't be any quibbling over which pair belongs to whom."

All the women around Emma laughed as they followed the sister into a room. "Be seated, ladies. The wounded arrive here by ambulance, stretcher, mule-drawn wagon, or carried by a buddy. Usually, they've received some basic bodily cleansing and treatment, such as bandaging of wounds, but not much else. Your job is to identify those who require more involved care than we can provide here, such as further surgery beyond the initial lifesaving measures." The sister stopped and looked around. "Any questions?" Emma noticed not one hand went up. *Thank goodness*, she thought. *Let's get this over with. We're all exhausted.*

The sister continued, "We have eight rooms in the school being used as wards, housing twenty-five patients in each room. These patients are seriously wounded, requiring intensive care prior to being moved out to a general hospital as soon as possible. A few will be heading to Brest to be sent directly home."

After a short pause, she continued, "Walking here you passed a tent area being used for less serious patients. We care for some three to four hundred in the tents until they return to the front. German planes bomb us whenever they please, so wear your helmets even while working inside. You never know when a bomb might go astray and hit the school. I advise you to also keep your gas masks with you at all times. You never know when you'll need them, especially when you take your turn up at the regimental aid station. I also want to warn you not to become softhearted and give your gas mask to a soldier who's lost his even if he's headed back to the front. You need that mask as much as he does, especially when we get patients who've been gassed and you must treat them. The gas clings to the wounded on their clothes and bodies. You can inhale enough gas while attending a patient to become gassed yourself. Remember, for your own sake, keep your gas masks."

After the hospital tour and a bite to eat, Emma and the others returned to their quarters. Exhausted from traveling, they did what was necessary before falling into bed. Some didn't even bother to undress, Emma included.

It began as a low rumble beneath her that grew louder, shaking the bed. Emma's eyes jerked open. Her brain yelled, *Earthquake! Surely lightening wouldn't strike twice, would it?!* She sat up and threw her legs over the side of the cot. Her heart raced as her feet felt a tremor in the wooden flooring. She heard a throaty "Ho!" followed by snickers. Emma's body relaxed as her mind translated the sounds as arriving animal-drawn ambulances.

Shoving her feet into already laced and tied shoes, she grabbed her apron and sweater as she strode toward the tent door. Stuffing her shoes into a pair of galoshes, she set out for the hospital. Through the dim light of the moon above, she made out several mule-drawn ambulances lined up in front. Corpsmen were already unloading the wounded and carrying them inside. Emma sloshed through the mud path as quickly as she could to the tune of slop-slop as she pulled her feet from the sucking mud.

Once inside, after boiling water over the primus stove, she set to work cleaning individual patients so the doctors could diagnose the severity of their wounds. Many already had bandages applied hastily around their wounds without having been cleaned, requiring a more thorough cleaning. All the blood, mixed with mud and other debris from the trenches, needed scrubbing from the patient, who probably hadn't had a bath in several weeks.

Some of the patients reached out to Emma calling, "Mama!" Others, whose eyes remained closed, whimpered like hurt toddlers. Many just stared into space, not giving any evidence of recognition of their surroundings.

When the time came for Emma's breakfast, the male corpsmen were left to finish up the bathing of the remaining patients, while she and the other nurses who'd already worked several hours walked to the mess hall. Her watch read 0700.

Going first to the tea area, Emma and Bev, a fellow American nurse, poured themselves mugs of hot tea to quench their thirst and warm their ice-cold hands. The kettle in which the tea was made astounded Emma. It was metal, not china, and enormous! Larger than any she'd seen on any ranch back home, but once a potful was made it served more than forty people with several cups without being refilled.

With their second mug of tea, Emma and Bev braved the breakfast line knowing exactly what they'd have: hot oatmeal with milk and a piece of toast, the only choice available. The cereal was warm but the toast cold and dry, having been grilled hours earlier. Bev, who came from a Scottish, home joked about calling the toast a "boardie" because that's what her father called cold toast that could be used several times over with several helpings of sweet jam toppings. Emma tried hard not to think of the warm tortillas or egg and sausage enchiladas she had at home.

After quenching their hunger, the two sat silently, each seeing the injured and hearing the sounds of their anguish in their heads. Emma couldn't forget the tiny flags on big toes identifying the leg to be amputated. The patients were all young, many still in their teens. Why aren't they back home attending school, dating girls, playing Rugby? It wasn't fair that they had to suffer such a lifetime loss.

Back on the ward, Emma discovered little had been done in her absence. With a smile on her face, she gathered up more hot water and cloths and set to work. The waste and mud had hardened since morning and scrubbing it away took more patience. With some, their military uniform soaked with fluid and caked with mud fused to their bodies with the feistiness of glue, Emma would have given anything for a warm tub of water to immerse them in. She watched as the young men tried not to yell out in pain, biting their lips until they bled while being treated.

When she recognized she'd maxed out her level of stoicism, Emma fled to the isolation of the storage room, cried, wiped her tears, and return to duty.

12

Days on the wards became routine: starting the primus stove so that water could be boiled, making beds in preparation for the incoming wounded, washing the newly arrived wounded, assisting the doctors with dressings, and giving loving attention to the patients. This last was personally very costly because it pulled at her heartstrings and involved her emotions. Her antidote was serving hot chocolate to any patients who could have it. How she wished her mama would have done the same while she grew up to ease her pain of rejection—made her a cup of cocoa. But she never did. Probably never thought of doing so because of her emotional detachment from her daughter, whom she saw as lacking in musical talent.

On Emma's one day off from duty, she haunted the small stores in town for cocoa. After she'd stripped them of all their cocoa, she searched the villages around. After pleading with her stepfather, he began to send her a regular supply. Jamie was delighted to do his part in supporting the war effort since he was too old to enlist and wouldn't have left her mama if he could. His letters often reminded her that once true love is found, it never should be ignored. That always brought tears to Emma's eyes. She prayed constantly for Wolfe's safety—he was now stationed at an aide station near the furthermost trenches.

"Emma, now that we don't have to search the countryside for cocoa, do you suppose we could try some French food at the café in town?" asked Bev.

Looking up from her letter writing, Emma nodded agreement. "Perfect timing," exclaimed Emma, folding her letter and slipping it into an envelope. "I'll mail my letter while we're in town."

Emma and Bev found the café almost deserted as they entered; only a couple of American officers were seated at a table near the back. One of them glanced up, then rose and walked toward them. "Ladies, would you like to join us? We haven't talked to American women since arriving." Laughingly, he added, "Bet you haven't ever heard that come-on?"

Both Emma and Bev felt their faces flush. Finally, Bev, after glancing at Emma, answered, "Of course we'd love to join you. Can't turn down an invitation like that."

As the captains held out the chairs for Emma and Bev to sit, they introduced themselves as Steve, holding Emma's chair, and Wes, short for Westley, holding Bev's chair. Once all were seated, Steve added, "I'm from Tennessee—my accent probable told you—and Westley is from Georgia."

"We figured you were from the South," answered Bev, grinning from ear to ear while Emma nodded agreement. "What brings you here? A day off from the trenches?"

"No," drawled Wes, "we're on our way to the front."

"Yes, we just stopped to indulge in a hot meal served at a table," replied Steve, suddenly wiping any merriment from his face. Shifting his feet, he leaned back against his chair as he glanced around for the waiter. Looking across at both women, he softly asked, "And what brings you both to town? A day off?"

Emma looked across at the young officer's smooth-shaven face with two dimples on each side of his cheeks. *He's so clean compared to the young patients I've been facing lately—and shaven too*, she thought. Composing herself, she answered, "Yes, Bev and I have a few hours from the hospital."

"So, you're both nurses. I didn't know we had any Americans over here."

Fingering her white napkin, Emma, without looking up, said, "Yeah, we're the first contingent to arrive after the declaration of war."

"Wow, I'm not certain even General Pershing is aware of any Army nurses being on French soil. We thought they were all sent to Britain for training."

Looking up into Steve's light blue eyes flecked with yellow, Emma solemnly said, "We disembarked in Liverpool, sailing to Brest on a British ambulance ship because of the urgent need of nurses."

"Yes, we heard about the nurse shortage. The British can't recruit enough volunteers. Even the Dutch and the French are strapped. The war's been going on too long."

Nodding, Bev absently straightened the white table cloth at her place before looking up. "We've encountered a couple of the English volunteers. They're helpful with the British wounded with their thick accents."

"Let's not talk war," suggested Wes. "Where are you two from? I don't recognize either one of you accents."

"Oh, that's easy—I'm from Idaho," said Bev and, pointing at Emma, added, "She's from New Mexico but has spent time in Texas and Idaho so she's homogenized."

With that remark, laughter filled the small café as the waitress approached with their meals.

For a while, silence descended on the table as they ate. The waiter refilled their cups with "thanks" being voiced by all. As one by one they all finished and sat back feeling satisfied, Emma said, "You mentioned you're attached to General Pershing. In what way are you working for him? Can you tell us?"

Wes folded his napkin carefully and replaced it on the table.

Looking up at her, she smiled and with his right hand indicated that their assignment wasn't to be discussed. Emma nodded and asked, "By any chance, were you with the general when he went down to the Mexican border to run the Mexican Army across the international line?"

"Oh, yes, both of us were with the contingent of troops who rode the train through Texas and down to the New Mexico border," answered Wes. "And we traveled with him when the president recalled us because he wasn't going to lead us into fighting both Mexico and Germany."

"Oh, I hadn't thought of that," Bev said, smiling at the waiter who was filling her water glass.

"Do you happen to know a Ben Zeiger with General Pershing?" asked Emma, watching Steve carefully.

"Yes, I know him." Standing up, Steve pushed his chair up. "He's with the general's staff. Nice guy for a Nebraska German American family, I believe. We all gave him a hard time until he proved himself. How do you know him?"

"On, we met on the ship coming over," answered Emma.

"Anyone for a walk? I think Wes and I have an hour before departure." Bev and Emma nodded and rose from the table, joining the two lieutenants. In pairs, they walked along the narrow cobblestone walk, looking in the store windows. They didn't encounter many townspeople but did pass a few French soldiers holding hands with their sweethearts and a few English sisters enjoying a few hours off from their duty. Emma noticed Bev and Wes deep in conversation as they walked holding hands. Emma looked up at Steve but he appeared deep in thought and happy to just have a walking companion.

"Wes, I think it's time for us to head to our pickup spot," said Steve hastening his steps.

Turning around, Wes stopped, dropped Bev's hand and stepped

into the street. "Yes, I guess you're right. In fact, we may be a little late." Nodding to both girls he said, "Thanks for a lovely afternoon. Sorry we have to rush."

Emma and Bev stood watching as the two young officers scurried toward the train depot. "Surely they're not going by train?" Emma said, "The last one left hours ago." Just then, they heard the rattle of a mule-drawn wagon approaching the depot. "No, I guess they're going by 'shanks mare' to the front lines," commented Emma. Turning, the two headed out of town toward the hospital as several ambulances passed them heading toward a station hospital further away from the fighting.

"Guess what we're going to be doing when we return?" asked Emma. "And your first two guesses don't count!".

Bev sighed, "More dirty beds to strip and clean beds to make for the next group of wounded. It's endless!"

13

Emma and Bev walked into their quarters to find four new residents, all from the United States. "Jackie!" shouted Emma, rushing over for a hug. "When did you all get here? What a surprise!"

"Pleased to see me?" asked Jackie, hugging Emma in return and gesturing toward the other new residents. "This is Frankie, Pinkie, and Virginia. We haven't been here long, perhaps half an hour. I thought I recognized your stuff over there. They didn't tell us who the other American nurses in this tent were, just that you were from the States."

"Welcome, welcome to our home away from home," greeted Emma and Bev in unison.

"Wow! Bev and I haven't been gone three hours and look at the wonderful changes."

As the six nurses walked into the first of the four wards assigned to them, all was quiet. The beds were empty but in disarray: blankets thrown back and pillows helter-skelter. Sighing, Emma said, "Well, ladies, we have our work cut out for us."

"Must the beds be made up immediately or can we have our dinner first?" asked Pinkie. "We haven't eaten since early this morning in Paris."

"Afraid we must," said Emma as she attacked the nearest bed. "We don't know when the next wave of wounded will arrive. Have to be ready."

"I'll check our supply of bandages and drugs," volunteered Bev walking toward the rear of the ward.

"Okay, but hurry back to help with the cleanup," called Emma, watching Bev disappear. Looking around at the other weary nurses struggling to tidy the beds, she thought of how tired she'd been upon arriving. Straightening up after making a cot, she asked loudly, "Any of you for a cup of cocoa?"

The resounding, "Yes!" didn't surprise Emma. Her secret tonic worked its magic. The beds in all four wards stood ready for new occupants just before the last call for supper. All was in readiness for the usual nightly arrival of newly wounded.

Soon after midnight, the sound of hooves woke Emma, signaling the arrival of wounded. Forcing first one eye open and then the other, she tried to convince herself she was dreaming but her ears told her differently. Boosting herself up on one elbow to a sitting position, she stood up, feet slipping into her waiting shoes. Grabbing her dress, she slipped it on before reaching the end of her bed and grabbed her sweater, helmet, and gas mask. Quick-stepping down the aisle of beds, she stumbled into her galoshes, shoved her helmet onto her head, and left the tent. Thank goodness it wasn't raining—only the quagmire of mud underfoot reminded her of the god-awful rain they'd been having.

The night was pitch black with no moon, thank goodness: any light gave the German flyers targets. Only a few stars shown above the trees around the makeshift hospital, once the village school. Slipping and sliding through the mud, Emma made her way to the hospital. At the entrance, she dodged corpsmen navigating the wounded inside. Cries, moans, and angry shouts greeted her. Close by she saw Captain Myers bending over a patient. She hurried to his side. The soldier lay wide eyed, grasping for breath, his entire chest openly exposed. As the doctor turned to leave, his eyes spoke: there was no saving this one. Emma covered the man's upper body with a blanket and followed the doctor.

One by one down the line of beds, the doctor checked the

wounded. Some only needed their bandages redone after applying antiseptic ointment. Others the doctor rebandaged himself. A few required stitches. There were a few injured who had flags around their big toes indicating possible amputation. Captain Myers inspected these cases carefully because if done at the casualty clearing station, errors often occurred. Those soldiers, knowing what the flag meant, always begged, "Please don't take off my leg." In a lot of these cases, gangrene had already set in so there was little hope, but most doctors tried. In a few cases, they succeeded in saving the limb.

When there was a surgery, Emma, being the only one with surgical experience, assisted. She was also responsible for preparing the surgery: firing up the primus stove, heating the needed water, checking to see that all the instruments were sterilized, and setting out the instruments and medicines required. In many cases, she also acted as anesthesiologist if a doctor wasn't available. After surgery, she cleaned up, readying for the next case.

Nursing during wartime meant providing tenderness, comfort, love, and courage. Many cried out for their mothers, needing to be held and a mother's comforting words of assurance and love. Some, who knew that death beckoned, asked her to recite the Lord's Prayer or the Twenty-Third Psalm. Usually, she held hands with the patient as she spoke the familiar words she'd memorized long ago as a child. It never failed, but saying the Psalm especially, always brought tears to her eyes.

When Emma entered the mess hall for dinner, she spotted a couple of the new nurses clustered together silently eating. They probably needed to mentally adjust to the horrors of war they were experiencing. She recalled how it had been with her.

Waiting in line to pick up a tray, she smelled "bully beef" as the English called it, a vegetable stew with bits of beef boiled to the point of oblivion. Why no mutton, she wondered? Didn't the British raise lots of sheep?

Collecting her mug of strong tea, she headed for the table where Captain Myers sat, concentrating on his knitting. "May I sit down with you?" she asked.

Looking up from his needles and wool, he said, "Of course, have a seat. Glad to have the company."

Emma settled down at the table with her tray. The plate on the other tray on the table still held a thick slice of bread, and an empty mug. "Is that all you're having for dinner?" she asked.

"Hum, no, I was waiting for you to join me." Putting down his knitting, Dr. Myers scooted up to the table, smiled at Emma, and took up his fork. "You finished up early."

"Well, there wasn't much to it," replied Emma, braking her bread into pieces. Stopping, she tilted her head to one side and asked, "How many times have you reused that wool of yours?"

Looking solemn, he finished chewing a bite before saying, "Oh, probably a dozen or so times. Why?"

"I know you knit to keep your fingers nimble for surgery but why don't you knit socks or scarves, something useful?"

"I didn't bring enough wool to do much with."

Emma took a bite of stew before making a comment. "Back in the States, women all over are knitting socks, scarves, and caps to send over here. My mama wrote the other day that many Navajo women are busy knitting for the war effort, as well as buying lots of war bonds. Walking around the square in Santa Fe the other day, she saw our Navajo women busy knitting while waiting to sell their blankets and jewelry. I'll bet I could get Mama to send wool over for you. There's plenty available in Santa Fe. Would you like that?"

"Certainly, that would be great."

14

As 1918 arrived, the United States' involvement in the war increased. Emma encountered fewer English doctors and more of her own countrymen. She saw an increase of American casualties. Her routine remained the same: making beds for new arrivals, stripping beds of those being sent to the station hospital, assisting doctors with dressings, making gallons of cocoa, pretending to be mother or sweetheart for the delirious, comforting all the others, and assisting in the surgery. The only variation in the routine was when they headed to the front for trench foot examination.

Arriving at the safe zone during rest time, the soldiers sat in rows, their bare feet stretched out in front ready to be checked. The nurses walked along the line checking each foot carefully for signs of gangrene, redness or blueness much like frostbite, or any impairment in feeling. Trench foot was serious business, but the first time Emma was confronted with the sight of outstretched naked toes, a bubble of laughter almost escaped her lips. Her fingers itched to go down the line of somber faced men tickling each bare foot. Of course, she controlled her growing bubble of laughter and inspected each foot with professional precision until the last foot. Looking up into the solemn youthful face, she saw a challenging twinkle in dark brown eyes. That did it for Emma. After inspecting between his toes, a few fingers brushed along his instep. The young man jerked back, swallowed a giggle, and flashed a big grin.

"Did I just see you tickle your last patient?" asked Jackie.

"Yes, you did," Emma answered. "He asked for it."

"Wish I'd had the nerve to do that. I love to tickle people, especially their feet."

"Well, next time we come to inspect, you can do it too," quipped Emma.

Pinkie, overhearing the conversation said, "How could you see anything enticing about all those smelly feet? The stench was unbelievable. I wanted to threw up."

Looking at Pinkie, Emma and Jackie said in unison, "What odor? We didn't smell a thing," bursting into laughter.

Emma dragged herself out of bed as she heard the day shift returning. She and Jackie had been assigned to the night shift for the last two weeks and neither of them had adjusted well to the change in sleeping and working hours. Having to eat at different times also didn't help the adjustment. Fumbling in the dark, she slipped into her uniform and grabbed her galoshes. Yips! They were on the wrong feet! She plunked her helmet on her head and headed for the hospital. It was dark as Hades but she'd traveled the path often, so her feet seemed to know the way. Entering the first ward, Emma stopped dead in her tracks. The ward was a mess. Pillows on the floor, blankets tangled with sheets, and bloody bandages everywhere.

Striding purposely toward the sound of laughter at the end of the ward where the nurses' station was, Emma found the corpsmen, now all Americans who had replaced the English corpsmen several weeks ago, standing around talking and enjoying coffee and cookies. "When do you plan to clean up the ward?" she demanded. No one paid any attention to her. In a louder voice she repeated the question: "When do you plan to clean up the ward? The ambulances will be arriving and we must be prepared."

Suddenly all was silent. A sturdy-looking corpsman with

reddish hair turned toward her. "We don't take orders from you or any nurse," smirked the young soldier. "We all outrank you in this man's Army." Turning toward his fellow corpsmen, who nodded assent, he added, "Clean up your own ward, WOMAN!" Then, the radish-top corpsman and his cohorts walked off the ward.

Seething with anger, Emma turned to Jackie, who was just entering the ward. "Did you hear that?" asked Emma.

"Just the last part," replied Jackie. "I've heard our countrymen don't respect us but this is a first. He vocalized it openly. How rude! Since we hold no rank, they don't think they have to obey any orders we give."

As Emma began stripping beds and cleaning up, she commented, "Why didn't our government give us any rank when they founded the Army Nurse Corps? That doesn't make any sense."

"Don't try making sense of how our federal government thinks and acts. There's no rhyme or reason to it. It only makes sense to men. We women can't even vote yet in the United States but black men can. Lincoln saw to that. Men still consider us inferior to them, the jackasses," commented Jackie gathering up dirty sheets.

The nurses had barely finished getting the ward ready when they heard the clatter of ambulance wagons arriving. Fortunately, the day shift had arrived and Emma and Pinkie, after giving their morning report to the next shift, hurried off to breakfast and bed but not before learning that most of the incoming wounded were French and Belgian. The "Boche," as the French and British called the Germans, had inflicted heavy casualties on their sector during the night, thanks to a full moon providing light to see movement in No-Man's-Land and the allied trenches.

Emma prepared for bed, but not before offering up prayers. "Please, Lord, keep Wolfe safe. Put your armor around him during battle and let no harm come to him. Keep his mind sharp for the healing work he must do. Stand with him at all times and guide him in all that he does. Amen." Emma fell onto her cot with visions of her golden-haired, blue-eyed betrothed, saying, "Good night, sweetheart. Love you mucho."

◇

During one meal, Emma sat at a table of very excited French nurses talking about an *Escadrille Lafayette* pilot hero named Eugene Bullard who'd visited the French wounded at the hospital. "Didn't you get to meet him?" asked one of the nurses.

"No," answered Emma, puzzled why she would be interested in meeting a French pilot.

"But," replied the nurse, "Eugene Bullard is an American from your Georgia. He's been a pilot since August 1917 flying his SPAD S.VII aircraft with a picture of a dagger stuck in a bleeding heart and the phrase *Tout sang qui coule est rouge,* which means 'all blood that runs is red.'"

"Never heard of him," replied Emma, shaking her head. "Why is he flying for the French rather than us?"

"I've heard the rumor that your government won't let African Americans join the Air Force," came a reply from across the table.

"I'm afraid America's still a very prejudiced country. Our black troops are segregated into their own units with white officers. The American Indian wasn't considered a citizen nor even an immigrant, legal or otherwise, until one draft board, to fulfill their enlistment quotas, decided to declare them eligible. After that, some draft boards began to recruit them so now there are Native American units." With that, Emma rose from the table and left feeling proud of herself for speaking up.

15

Emma had finished reciting the Twenty-Third Psalm when there was a tap on her shoulder. "You have a visitor to see you," the orderly said. "He's waiting outside."

Standing up, she nodded to the young corpsman. *Who's asking for me? It must be bad news if I have to go outside.* She felt her heart quicken as heat spread through her body. Hastening her steps, she stepped outside. No one stood close. *Where is my visitor?* she wondered.

"Emma, over here."

Jerked toward the voice, she saw a silhouette standing next to a horse. "Wolfe?" she cried. As she rushed forward, she stopped. It wasn't Wolfe. "Juan? What are you doing here?" She felt a heaviness in her chest. "Has something happened to Wolfe?"

Reaching out, Juan took her hand. "He's missing, Emma. The dressing station was overrun several days ago. We don't know what's happened to Wolfe. We haven't even been able to retake the facility. I came as soon as I could to tell you."

Emma slumped toward Juan, who caught her as Pinkie appeared near the door motioning him inside.

While Pinkie looked for smelling salts, Juan held her, whispering, "I'll find him. Don't you worry. I wrangled the assignment to find him. I'll bring him back to you. Trust me."

After a few whiffs, Emma regained consciousness. Opening her eyes, she looked around and sneezed but didn't speak. Pinkie was about to give her another whiff of smelling salts, but Emma waved her off. Taking big breaths of air, she gave Juan a pleading look as he settled her in a chair.

Pinkie turned to Juan. "What did you say to her?"

Straightening his shoulders, Juan scowled. "I'm Juan, a longtime friend." Turning back to where Emma sat, he explained, "I came to tell her that Wolfe, her fiancé, is missing."

"Well, you didn't do it in a gentle manner."

Emma raised a hand toward Pinkie and shook her head.

"See what you've done?" said Pinkie in a blustery tone. "She's lost her voice."

"This has been a shock, I know, but better from me than a stranger," muttered Juan. Squatting down in front of the chair, he took her hand. "Emma, I'll find him for you. They couldn't have taken him far and, as a surgeon who speaks German, they'll make use of him. I've heard they're short of doctors at the front lines."

Emma's frightened eyes met Juan's jet-black ones. She gave his hand two squeezes, their childhood signal of love and encouragement. The wood planking under Juan creaked as he stood up. "I'm off to our trench area to search. Get some rest. Keep us in your prayers. I'll be back as soon as I have any news," said Juan smiling down at her. Turning to Pinkie, he said, "Take care of her for me."

Emma turned her head away from Juan's receding back, letting the tears flow. *Oh, Wolfe, come back to me. I need you. Use your crafty Texan skills to evade the Huns.* Taking the handkerchief held out to her, Emma wiped away her tears and blinked away more forming. Opening her mouth, she tried to say something to Pinkie but nothing came out. She'd lost her voice, just like when she was ten after the earthquake. How embarrassing to have this happen!

The Chief Nurse, after hearing about Emma's fiancé, ordered her to her quarters, saying, "You take it easy now, and try to rest. By the time you wake up, your voice will have returned. It's the shock of hearing about Wolfe. Don't worry, with a little rest you'll be fine. Later, Pinkie will bring you a nice cup of tea."

Events went on about Emma as she lay in bed, not registering what was going on until morning, when she felt something small jump up on her bed. It purred and nestled close to her chest. Reaching out, she felt fur. Her eyes popped out. What was on her bed? Glancing down, she saw the upturned wee pink nose of a black, gray, and white cat. Smiling, Emma slid her hand out from under the covers and stroked the soft fur. "Where did you come from?" she asked. "Oh, my goodness, kitty poo, my voice is back. You brought it back." Smiling to herself, Emma lay there stroking the cat and enjoying the warmth and loud purring. Somehow, she felt content and peaceful. "Yes, Lord, thank you for sending me a sign that Wolfe will be found."

Looking around at all the empty cots, Emma jumped up and dressed. Fearing she was late, she ran out of the tent, almost colliding with Jackie, who blurted out, "Why are you in a hurry?"

Emma stopped dead in her tracks. "I'm late," she laughed. "I'm late for a very important date."

"Oh, what would that be, Miss Prissy?" chuckled Jackie.

"My job. Have you noticed? I've got my voice back! All is right for today."

"Well, that was a remarkable recovery. I guess Thomas the Tom worked his magic on you."

"You know about the cat?" asked Emma.

Nudging her way around Emma, a tentmate, Jackie said as she entered the quarters, "One of the British Sisters gave him to us yesterday because we've been having mouse problems and they couldn't feed two cats. So we took him. Isn't he adorable?"

Jackie glanced across the table at Emma. "That was a handsome lieutenant who saved you when you swooned yesterday. Is he in the medical corps? I didn't recognize his brass."

Finishing the bite she had in her mouth before answering, Emma said, "No. Juan is in the Veterinary Corps. He's a veterinarian."

"That's interesting, I didn't know there were animal doctors fighting in the war."

Nodding, Emma continued, "And for your edification, no, he doesn't have a girlfriend."

"It looks like he spends a lot of time on horseback. Is that what his job entails?"

Shoving her tray away from in front of her, Emma put her elbows on the table. "Yes, I think he rides daily, first to accustom horses to battle noises and also to help the injured horses recover so they can return to duty. I was surprised to see him because the last I heard, he was assigned to an advanced remount station where there was a large number of horses and mules to train."

"That was a beautiful bay horse he rode in on. I noticed it hitched over by the corner of the hospital."

Catching Jackie's eye, Emma replied, "Juan has always loved good horse flesh. I'll bet he's chosen the best of the lot for himself."

"Do you think he may have known about your fiancé's disappearance before anyone else?" asked Jackie.

"Maybe so."

As they walked back to their quarters, Jackie continued asking questions of Emma. "Are there American horses over here or do they just use French horses?"

"Juan told me they're having to ship both mules and horses over because neither the French nor the British can supply enough. The war has gone on too long. It has depleted the available horse flesh."

Chuckling, Jackie asked, "I wonder if our horses have a preference for their own countrymen?"

"Oh, Jackie, only you would come up with a question like that!"

16

The monotony of Emma's days blended together as she awaited word about Wolfe. Arriving for duty, she faced the patients transported to the hospital directly from the battlefield. There were horrible chest or stomach wounds, shattered limbs, and disfigured faces. Most wounds had been bandaged either by the patient himself or at an aid station close to the trenches. Emma dreaded removing these bandages for fear of pulling off the dried blood or scabs, thus opening up the wound to hemorrhage. In these cases, she arranged tubes of hypochlorite of soda solution to run down to the wounds from a jar hung above the patient's bed. The solution known as Carrel Dakin solution, so named after the two doctors who discovered it, killed the microbes or bacilli in the wounds and helped to shorten the recovery time.

One day she arrived to discover a patient in desperate need of procedure. Knowing what the doctor would require, Emma went to start boiling the water to sterilize the instruments he would need. She found a pair of rubber gloves being sterilized in their only receptacle. Knowing that time was of the essence, she removed the gloves, replaced the water and set the instruments to be sterilized. Upon returning to get the instruments, she discovered they'd been replaced by the rubber gloves. Starting over again, she was confronted by an English volunteer aide of the nobility who demanded the gloves be done first. Emma told her a patient's life was at stake but was rebuked because as the Englishwoman insisted, she wasn't "going to be late for a date with a doctor." Emma won but not until the English doctor intervened. He cancelled the date.

It had been a long day, fourteen hours to be exact. Emma was making her last check of her patients when she heard, "Nurse, could I have a drink of water?" Stopping, she looked around and saw young Steven motioning to her.

Emma smiled at the boy and walked toward his bed. "Of course, you may have a drink," she said, as she held him up so he could sip from the glass. "Take another sip, Steven, you haven't had much liquid today. You've got to drink more so you get better."

"Am I going to get better?"

"You did a fine job after the aide dog found you and you tended to your own wound. I couldn't have done any better." Watching Steven lean back on his pillow after a second sip of water, Emma smiled at the drawn face of the youth. She tried not thinking that he probably wouldn't make it through the night.

"Nurse, would you mind saying the Twenty-Third Psalm for me. I think it will help me sleep."

Emma nodded, "Of course I'll recite it for you."

> *The Lord is my shepherd; I shall not want; He maketh me to lie down in green pastures: He leadeth me beside still waters. He restoreth my soul: He leadeth me in the paths of righteousness for his name's sake. Yea, though I walk through the valley of the shadow of death, I will fear no evil: for thou art with me; thy rod and thy staff, they comfort me.*

Emma stopped. Steven's hand had slipped off her arm, his face calm and at peace. She felt his wrist for a pulse. Crossing herself as the sisters had taught her in school, Emma pulled the sheet up over Steven's young face. Standing up, she swallowed a howl and headed for the door. Stumbling, with tears flooding her eyes, she walked toward her tent. The sound of an airplane overhead sent her eyes suddenly skyward. The bright moonlit night showed the hospital and all the tents around it. "No, no, not tonight," she shouted as she ducked back into the safety of the hospital. Breathing heavily, she squatted down and started praying, "Lord, don't let him see us."

Legs shaking from her awkward position, Emma placed her head between her bent knees expecting to hear the whiz of bullets. As minutes passed, the sound above grew fainter. Emma raised her head as she took a breath. The hospital had been spared. Looking upward she whispered, "Thank you, Lord."

"Hurry up Emma, they won't wait for us," shouted Jackie as she walked down the row of cots toward the door.

"I'm coming as fast as I can," answered Emma. Cramming one last piece of clothing into her bag and taking a last look around to see that she hadn't left anything, she headed for the door but stopped, hearing a loud meow. Turning, she spotted Thomas the Tom on Pinkie's bed. "We'll be back in three days, sweetie. We're off to Paris. You keep the mice and rats at bay while we're gone and we'll bring you a whole fish of your own."

Every compartment on the Paris train appeared filled as Emma, Pinkie, and Bev ran along looking for empty seats. Near the end of the train they found space.

"I can't believe we're on our way to Paris and not just passing through," Bev said.

Breathlessly, Pinkie plopped down in a seat. "It's going to be great, Paris. My family back home won't believe me when I write them." Suddenly, a freckled face turned toward her.

"Why won't your family believe you about going to Paris?" asked the bemused uniformed soldier beside her.

"Lawson Edwards!" shrieked Bev, throwing her arms around him. "What are you doing here?"

"Same as you, I suspect. Fighting for Uncle Sam and the good old U S of A."

"Emma, Pinkie, this is my good friend Lawson from back home," announced Bev with her hand still on his shoulder.

"How long have you been in France?" asked Emma glancing at the silver bars on his shoulders and recognizing him as a first lieutenant. Wolfe, being a captain, wore two attached silver bars on each epaulet.

"Oh, we've been here six months or more," Lawson replied. "When we get to Paris, let me introduce you to my friends Marshall and Stew. We met at Fort Bragg during training. We're headed to Paris on leave for a few days. How about you all?"

"We are too—that is, we have leave too," replied Bev, gazing at Lawson.

"Bev, do you and your friends have plans while you're here?" asked Lawson as he helped her down from the train.

"No, we're just sightseeing—well, all expect for Emma. She wants to visit friends at the American embassy and take in a concert or two."

As Stew and Marshall helped Pinkie and Emma alight from the train, Stew asked, "If you ladies like, why not join us in touring Paris? We'd love to act as your escorts."

Bev and Lawson turned around and faced the other two couples. With a twinkle in her eye, Bev said, "What fun! Let's do it! And I bet there're places we need male escorts."

After checking into the hotel, Emma left Bev and Pinkie, who raced off to meet Lawson and Stew as she headed for the American embassy to locate Tom and Bob. As she walked along the busy street, she felt like she was walking on air because of not having to wear her galoshes. There was no mud on the streets of Paris.

At the first street intersection, she felt a hand grab her, preventing her from walking straight into oncoming traffic. "Wow! I must be careful, there's traffic!" The streets seemed monstrously wide compared to the village streets that only allowed horses pulling carts in tandem. Gazing at the ornate features of the buildings and shops as she walked by was overpowering. Emma had never seen such embellishment on buildings. It was all so overwhelming! Finally, she found herself in front of the embassy.

"Emma, you found us!" greeted Bob and Tom, walking toward her. "We've been watching for you," said Tom, opening his arms and giving her a hug along with cheek kisses, then handing her over to Bob for a similar greeting.

"What a welcome sight you two are," said Emma, stifling her emotions.

Bob, holding her at arm's length, asked, "What's the problem? How can we help?"

Emma's face crumbled and tears flowed despite her effort to control them. She felt arms guiding her into the embassy. Helped to a chair in a tiny room off the lobby, two concerned faces stare at her. "Now what has happened? How can we help?"

Looking at neither man directly but staring at the floor, she replied, "I need help in locating Wolfe. He's disappeared from the dressing station. The Germans overran it, from what I've been told. He remained behind or was left for some reason. Wolfe wasn't there when the French and Americans took it back." Looking at Bob first and then Tom, Emma said, "No one can tell me what happened to Wolfe. I hope you can find out for me."

The two young men looked anxiously at each other. This was a tall order she'd plunked in their laps. And risky, too. They'd never divulged that both were in the spy business—actually no one at the embassy except their chief in London knew. Tom, stooping down on his haunches in front of Emma, took one hand and looked into her eyes, saying, "This is a little out of our league as communications officers, but we'll see if we can find out anything from our contacts."

"Meanwhile," said Bob, "Let's have some fun while you're in Paris. Tom has to work tonight but I have tickets to a concert just as you requested in your letter."

Wiping the tears away with a handkerchief offered, Emma nodded, "Sounds great."

Tom moved to help Emma up. "Tomorrow night's mine while Bob works. I have tickets to a violin concert. How's that for planning? We American doughboys know how to show a gal a good time while in Paris. Of course, both nights include dinner."

"You two are something!"

"Just something?" quizzed both in unison.

"Something very special," answered Emma with a broad grin.

"Okay, enough of this," said Bob guiding Emma toward the door. "We have places to go and things to see."

"Don't keep her out too late," yelled Tom after them. "I've planned a pretty busy day for us tomorrow."

Emma returned to her hotel room early according to her mental clock. As the first one back, she had the pick of beds so she took the one farthest from the door and the bathroom, knowing that she'd probably be the earliest in each night. Slipping into bed, she tossed and turned as she went over all the possible situations as to what might have happened to Wolfe. Had he been captured? Had he escaped capture? Had he been wounded and taken to a hospital? Or had he fooled the Germans into thinking he was one of them? He spoke German fluently but could he get by with his Texas accent? Mulling these scenarios over, she hoped somehow Tom and Bob would be able to uncover some answers.

Although Tom and Bob had never revealed what their job in communications entailed at the embassy, Emma understood the underlying message the two gave that she wasn't supposed to ask, so she didn't. Now she hoped that, somehow, they had access to confidential information about troops on the front lines. Turning onto her side, she thought about visiting the Red Cross headquarters the next day before meeting up with Tom.

Pinkie and Bev were sound asleep as Emma slipped from her bed the next morning. She didn't know when they'd gotten back. She must have been dead to the world. Tiptoeing around, she dressed and headed to the café across the street from the hotel. Settling down at an outside table, she ordered coffee and blintzes, French pancakes, that she'd discovered she loved while in Brest. It was quite early, but the number of people hurrying by surprised her. As she savored her breakfast, she found herself fascinated by how elegantly dressed the women were compared to the plainly dressed village women. Looking down at her uniform, she realized she must look very dowdy to everyday Paris citizens. Embarrassed, she pulled her feet further under the table. Her military shoes, so sensible and sturdy, were scuffed and dingy. What must Tom and Bob think of her?

"Emma, over here," came a call as she raced along the sidewalk heading for the embassy. She'd lost track of time as she engaged in people watching. Tom had mentioned their doing some sightseeing before dinner, a visit to a museum, and then the violin concert in the evening. Emma was really looking forward to the string performance. Her fingers fairly tingled at the thought of hearing a violin played again. How she missed her own instrument. Waving in the direction of Tom, Emma quickened her pace and headed in his direction.

"Hello!" greeted Emma, planting a kiss on each side of Tom's face and receiving the same from him.

"Ready for some exploring? I've planned a big day for us. And guess what? Bob is going to join us for our late-night supper after the concert. He may have some information for you about Wolfe by then. Keep your fingers crossed."

17

Emma gazed out the window as the train chugged out of Paris returning her to her duty station. Although physically refreshed from the two days of vacation, mentally she was in the same frame of mind as when she arrived—worried. Bob and Tom hadn't been able to obtain any news concerning Wolfe's location or if he was still alive. Her trip to the Red Cross hadn't produced anything either. Pictures of her beloved crowded in upon her. She whispered upward to the sky and clouds passing by, "Please, God, let him be alive and come back to me."

"Did you say something?" asked Bev, who sat beside her.

"No, nothing important," Emma answered, shaking her head as she turned toward her friend. Pinkie, Lawson, and Stew sat across from them crammed into one seat meant for two. They were laughing and joking around, sharing the good times they'd had at some dance hall the night before. Emma turned back to look out the window at the rolling green fields and blue sky. Having grown up mostly around mountains, she felt very unprotected without any, almost as if she could slip off the earth and into the wide-open space of the universe.

Reaching their destination all too soon, the three nurses said their "goodbyes to Marshall and Stew and hopped on the small wagon sent from the hospital to carry them and their luggage up to the old converted school. As Emma trudged toward their tent, she fell silent, just like her other two companions. Thoughts of returning to duty forced them back to facing the horror of war.

Thomas the Tom met them as they entered. Mewing and purring loudly, he escorted them, tail held high, to their cots. Emma's was the last. Thomas immediately jumped on hers and walked back and forth brushing his soft furry body against her. "What a wonderful welcome back, old boy." Looking around, she said, "Looks like you kept all the local vermin at bay. Good job," praised Emma, sitting down beside Thomas and stroking him from head to tail.

Emma continued on night duty upon returning from her two-day leave. "What a jolt," she said to the cat sprawled on her cot. After unpacking and going for a midday meal, she joined Thomas on her cot. Hopefully, she'd get enough shut-eye so she could manage the upcoming night shift. Darkness descended outside all too soon, and Emma headed for the wards assigned, all different than the ones she normally served.

Looking in on the first ward, she found only a few cases left behind. One patient she knew about, a young Frenchman wishing to escape the horrors of war, had shot himself in the shoulder. Unfortunately, the French military, who took a hard stand in such incidents, ruled that he'd intentionally shot himself. He'd face a firing squad just as soon as he recovered.

Down a couple of beds from him lay another young Parisian who'd had both legs amputated. His parents visited soon after his surgery and Emma had heard from one of the French nurses that he'd begged his papa to shoot him and put him out of his misery. Emma thought it was so sad that the two young men couldn't exchange places.

Midway through her shift, Emma, after servicing hot cocoa to the few remaining patients, sat down with a cup of tea. Since she'd been on leave, she'd missed the last issue of the *Stars and Stripes* newspaper published by the American Expeditionary Force. Eagerly, she scanned the paper for some hint of what might have happened to Wolfe. Nothing! Sipping her tea, she began reading various articles until one in particular caught her eye. The newspaper had started a campaign for units to adopt needy French children, which only cost eighty-eight dollars. The money was funneled through the Red Cross. Emma paused in her reading. *What a good idea!* she thought. How she wished she had the money to adopt a child, but the Army couldn't be relied upon to pay the nurses on a timely basis. Sometimes, they even went without getting paid and they never knew how much they'd receive. What little she was paid went for necessities, like soap. She envied the women in the auxiliary service who received a regular salary every month.

As the night hours crept along, Emma emptied bedpans, helped appease the thirst of patients, readjusted pillows, and assured frightened patients that the enemy wasn't attacking. As the hint of morning's light showed through the dusty windows, Emma heard the groaning of wagon wheels and hooves signaling the approach of another batch of wounded from the trenches. Her unhurried semipeaceful time in the wards was ending.

Stretchers arrived, filling the vacant beds in the wards. Emma and the corpsmen hurried from one bed to another, carefully stripping mud- and blood-caked uniforms from the wounded. Using the top blanket on the beds as washcloths, they gently cleaned the mangled bodies and removed any bandages so the doctors could ascertain the soldiers' medical needs. Once the patient's body was clean and his medical condition examined, his top blanket was replaced and he was moved to his clean bed underneath.

With a sigh of weariness, Emma saw that everyone was settled. She felt sluggish and empty of strength. *Will I make it to my tent?* she wondered. Clutching her sweater around her, she left the hospital and headed for her tent.

"Emma, wait. I need to tell you something," shouted Pinkie, running after her.

She turned toward her friend, almost falling. "What is it, Pinkie?"

Grabbing Emma's forearms to steady her, Pinkie stared into Emma's eyes. "We have a wounded Navajo soldier who's asking for you. He says he has a message for you."

Adrenaline shot through Emma, her body receiving a second wind. "Where is he? Take me to him."

Emma followed Pinkie back into the hospital and through first one ward and then another. Finally they reached the ward that Emma recognized as one of the gas wards.

"Here he is, over here," indicated Pinkie in a whisper. "Don't get too close—we still haven't removed his blanket ... It's laden with mustard gas."

Standing as close as allowed in gassed cases, Emma said, "Hello, I understand you asked for me. I'm Emma."

The young soldier turned his head and looked up. "Yes, I have a message from Juan for you. You do know who Juan is, don't you?"

"Yes, I know Juan. We grew up in New Mexico together."

The young Navajo swallowed, licked his lips, and fought for breath. "Juan says don't worry. Pray."

As Emma started to lean closer to the patient, Pinkie stopped her. They exchanged warning looks, and Emma moved back. "Where's Juan?" The question hung in the air. The patient's body had gone limp. His head sagged.

Pinkie caught her as she began to slump. "Oh, Emma, I'm so sorry. Thankfully you got here in time to hear his message."

Straightening, Emma nodded as her eyes misted over. "Yes, but I don't understand. How could this man know about my friendship with Juan? I thought most of the Navajos were stationed in Italy with the Army Veterinary Service."

"I've heard that that part of this Great War is over. He's probably been transferred up here. We certainly have enough mules and horses needing care. He's probably at the old French cavalry barracks called Quartier Margueritte near the towns of Saint-Mihiel and Verdun."

"How do you know that?" asked Emma.

Smiling shyly, Pinkie answered, "One of my old boyfriends is with the Veterinary Service in charge of the receiving area of injured horses."

"Do you suppose your friend might know where Juan's searching for Wolfe?"

Straightening her apron as she turned away from Emma, "He might. I'll ask."

"Oh, Pinkie, I hope so. I haven't heard from Juan in a long time."

18

Emma lay in her cot stroking Thomas, nestled beside her, purring and brushing his head against her hand. Looking up at the canvas above, she said in a mellow voice, "I do hope Juan has discovered Wolfe's whereabouts … It's been weeks since I learned of his disappearance. No one seems to know what happened to him. Why hasn't Juan sent me word? Where is Juan? Has he also gone missing?" Turning her head into the pillow, despairing that nothing mattered. She curled around Thomas and felt him relax into her chest. "That's right, my sweet," she said. "Listen to my broken heart."

The rain pelted down on the tent, rousing Emma from her fitful sleep. Turning on her back, she felt cold and damp. How she missed the dry heat of home. Slipping one hand out from under the covers as she glanced at her alarm, she cursed and threw the covers off as she jumped out of bed. "Crazy! I'm going to be late."

As she stepped into the hospital, Emma's foot slipped out from under her. Startled, she found herself flat on her back in the entrance. "OH!! NO!" Looking around to see who might have witnessed her fall, she saw no one but felt arms encircle her.

"Need a little help?" asked a male voice behind her.

Helped to her feet, Emma turned to see who her knight in shining armor could be. "Juan! Where have you been?!" squealed Emma, throwing her arms around him and almost upending both of them.

"Well, if it isn't my old New Mexico gal!" joked Juan. "Haven't you learned yet that the mud in this country is slippery?"

Stomping her foot, Emma poked Juan in the stomach. "Stop it. Have you found Wolfe?"

Turning serious, Juan took Emma's hand, guiding her to a bench in the lobby. "Let's sit."

Emma's face turned serious as she sat beside Juan. Searching his face, she tried to read what he was about to impart but couldn't. Her heart palpitated, her breathing rapid.

Juan reached for her hand, clasping it with both of his before giving a pat. "I do have some news for you but not much. Wolfe, as far as we know, hasn't been captured or found dead. Your friends at the American embassy, Tom and Bob, have been very helpful. In fact, they're the reason I've officially been assigned to find Wolfe."

"Oh, Juan, I'm so glad you're here," said Emma. "Just having you near eases my mind. You'll find him."

Reaching up, he stroked her cheek before saying, "I'll do my best. The command also assigned to me two Native Americans, both Navajo trackers." Squeezing her hand before releasing it, he stood and walked toward the door.

"I'll pray for you all," called Emma.

Life became rote for Emma. Work consumed her days and nights found her sleepless except when Thomas the Tom's warm body lay close enough so she could stroke his silky fur and listen to his rhythmic purring, which helped to lull her into dreamland.

"Come on, Emma, let's cross the Rio Grande here where it isn't very deep. Hold my hand—you know I won't let go of you. There's a lovely place on the other side for our picnic lunch. Don't worry. Come on, it will be fun," urged Wolfe, stretching out his hand toward her. As a child, she'd been warned never to wade in the Rio

Grande River and she never had, but now that she was a grown-up, surely it was safe. Besides, Wolfe was there with her. He wouldn't let anything bad happen to her. Laughing excitedly, she reached out for his hand. It was out of her reach, so she stretched further out. Reaching out her fingers even more, she touched his but she could not grasp his hand. Each time she tried, his hand seemed to move further away. Emma shot up in bed, shaken and terrified. It was the same dream every night! She couldn't reach Wolfe. "Lord, what are you trying to tell me?" Her mother always said dreams had meanings. What could be the meaning of her dream? Would she and Wolfe never to be together? "Oh, Lord, no, don't take my Wolfe away from me."

Nursing didn't take her mind off the search that was going on to locate Wolfe. She was moved to the gas ward. At first, she was so concerned about Wolfe that she failed to take adequate precautions to protect herself from the effects of gas. She'd been warned that the gas lingered on the clothing of the wounded and she could be gassed by breathing in too much while around a recently arrived patient. One American nurse, Helen Fairchild, had already died as a result of gas poisoning. Emma hadn't heeded the warning at the beginning of her tour on the ward and gotten a slight but dangerous case of gas overdose, spending a couple of days in the isolation section for nurses. Most of the women were nurses recovering from shell shock, nervous conditions, or exhaustion. Having liquids forced down her while hospitalized helped her to have more sympathy for her patients when she returned to the gas ward.

Working with gassed patients had its humorous moments. After a gas attack, there were always a few soldiers who claimed they were gassed but weren't. The standard operating procedure was to ask the patient if he'd like a meal. If their answer was yes, one would be brought to them. If a person had really experienced gassing, they couldn't and didn't want to eat, but a person not gassed would happily eat the entire meal set before them.

Two weeks had passed since Juan's visit, with no word from him. Emma frequently visited in the other wards hoping to pick up news from the front. Now, in the spring of 1918, the hospital received only wounded from the United States. Several American doctors were attached to the hospital, at least one from a western state. As often as possible, she and Pinkie tried to sit with him at meals so they could reminisce about back home. Another doctor, a surgeon, who was Pennsylvania Dutch, often joined them. Pinkie thought he was sweet on Emma, but she disagreed hardily because he frequently asked Emma to assist him in surgery.

One gratifying case involved a young soldier from the same Pennsylvania town as the doctor. By chance, the doctor recognized the young patient as he was going through the ward. He stopped to chat and, while talking, noticed that a ribbon was attached to his toe. The doctor examined the leg and decided that he thought he could save it. Normally, the soldier would have been automatically transferred to the next hospital to have his leg removed, but the doctor arranged to operate immediately, saving the leg.

One morning, as Emma got up from the table in the mess, she heard wagon wheels screech to a halt. Pulling the stray hairs back from her face, she headed for the hospital lobby, thankful that her ward time was up and she could head to her quarters. Stepping outside, she noticed a lone horseman at the rear of the ambulances. That's strange, she thought. Who could it be? As she turned toward her tent, she heard, "Emma, hold up."

Turning back, she squinted. Was she hallucinating? "Juan, is that really you?" she cried.

19

Emma sat across the table watching Juan shovel down corn beef hash and fried potatoes between gulps of coffee. While chewing, he'd look up at her, smile, swallow, and utter, "Good stuff," and then attack the mounts of food on his plate.

Although irritated that he was more interested in eating than divulging his news, Emma tried hard not to question him. It was obvious that he was starved. His usual lean face now showed every bone under a thin layer of skin. His usual shinning dark hair was matted and bore a film of yellowish dust much like that caked over the wounded when they arrived. His sparkling cinnamon eyes still held a glint, but Emma noticed dark bags under them.

With his plate scraped clean, Juan settled back in his chair. Cradling his third mug of coffee in both hands, he looked over at Emma. "Wow! That was the best meal I've had in days." Shifting his feet, stretched out under the table, he said, "Thanks for being patient with me. I know you're anxious to know if I've found Wolfe. The answer is maybe, I can't be certain. Jesus, my Navajo tracker is still behind the German lines near a little French town where we think he is."

"I don't understand," puzzled Emma, leaning toward Juan. "Why didn't you sneak in to make certain?"

"The town is heavily reinforced by the Germans, Emma. There was no way we could make certain, but we have spoken to a French farmer nearby who claims there's a German doctor under arrest in the town until he can be transferred to Berlin."

"But you haven't seen the prisoner, have you? So, you're not certain he's Wolfe?"

"No, neither Jesus nor I have."

"Why are you back here then?" asked Emma.

"I'm back to see General Pershing. I need further orders as to what he wants done."

Emma slapped her fist on the table saying, "But you can't just leave him there to be moved to Berlin, even if he isn't Wolfe. Perhaps he's a German American. He's in trouble. You need to help him. You know, don't you, that many of our soldiers, officers included, are German Americans, very loyal, may I say, to our county. You must help this person even if it isn't Wolfe."

"Hold on, Emma, I'm just as concerned as you are—that's why I'm back to see the General. I need orders, but most of all I need help. Perhaps a diversion, so Jesus and I can go in unnoticed and rescue him." Emma's body slacken and her shoulders slumped. Juan reached across the table taking her hand in his. "I'm doing all I can. Be patient. I have a good feeling about this. I truly feel this is Wolfe. We're going to free him."

Emma sucked in the bile in her mouth and nodded. She knew she couldn't ask for anything more. She had to trust Juan completely as she'd never done before.

The trench warfare continued as the weeks passed. The back and forth of who had taken which sections changed daily, making it difficult to keep track of units. The war wasn't going well for the allies but they were glad the United States had joined the fight. The influx of wounded increased and the number of American doughboys pained Emma. Most of the doctors at the hospital were now Americans, as were the nurses. German air raids increased with the warmer and clearer weather. Emma walked from her tent to the hospital without wearing galoshes but the wounded still arrived in their battle torn uniforms caked in sludge.

The fear of bomb attacks from German planes was constant with the advent of mild weather. So far they'd missed the hospital but not the tents around. Emma's tent had been hit early on, and she'd lost most of her clothing. Fortunately, Thomas the Tom had been out hunting when the tent was hit and retuned unscathed. Until replacement tents arrived, the nurses banded together, sharing quarters. Nighttime wasn't even safe from the enemy planes, especially if there was a full moon.

Even with the longer hours at the hospital and the fear of being bombed, Emma kept hoping and praying that Juan would bring Wolfe back to her. She still had nightly nightmares involving being left by him or not being able to reach him. Pinkie and Bev ate with her as often as they could to encourage her to eat. Emma lost her appetite and became a skeleton of her old self. Even Thomas the Tom must have noticed, because he started bringing her some of the tasty meaty morsels he caught, laying them next to her shoes at the side of her cot.

One morning, Emma was called in by the Chief Nurse. "Emma, I've got orders that you are to report to a hospital in Paris. I've had your bag packed and a special conveyance will be here shortly to drive you to Paris." Smiling, she handed Emma an envelope. "Here's your last months' pay. Good luck with your special assignment and hurry back to us. You'll be missed."

"But can't I say goodbye to everyone?" asked Emma as she watched the Chief Nurse stand, indicating she was dismissed.

"No, there is no time." And with that, Emma was rushed out the door, handed her bag, and walked to the front of the hospital.

A mud-spattered Bugatti sped Emma along the rut-plagued roadway to the outskirts of Paris before taking a side road. The driver and two other passengers hardly spoke at all. The driver focused on driving and the other two appeared exhausted, dozing intermittently during the drive. Emma, after observing her traveling companions and appreciative of their aloofness, watched the passing scenery deep in thought. She wished she knew the names of the wildflowers alongside of the road. They looked a lot like poppies and reminded her with their delicate colors and perkiness that life did continue thriving even during wartime. The trees stood straight and tall, proudly displaying their leafiness, not whipped blackish brown toothpicks from dropped bombs and gunfire.

Puzzled as to why she'd been ordered to report to a general hospital near Paris, she tried to come up with some logical reason. Had Tom or Bob at the American embassy pulled some strings to get her transferred? Were they short of surgical nurses? No, that couldn't be the reason. Maybe one of the surgeons she knew had requested her specifically—not likely, but possible.

The car stopped, jerking Emma from her thoughts. The car was parked in front of a multistoried building at the end of a circular drive. Her door opened and Emma looked into the smiling face of Tom, who offered his hand to help her from the car. "Welcome to Paris. Hope your trip was pleasant. Andrey, your driver, is the best the embassy can offer."

Her mind in a whirl, Emma was speechless as she allowed Tom to help her from the vehicle. Bob was there, reaching in for her bag. Although pleased to see them both, her head told her something wasn't right. Why were they meeting her at a general hospital? This trip wasn't for pleasure, was it?

Each man hooked one of her arms in his and lead her into the hospital. "We'll explain why you're here after we get settled in an office," said Bob.

"I imagine you're hungry too, so I've ordered a light meal and tea for you," added Tom, as he opened a side door through which Emma was escorted.

The room Emma found herself in appeared to be a fancy parlor furnished with couches, chairs and end tables stacked with magazines and books. On a low table in front of one of the couches sat a tray of sandwiches, cake, and a teapot with cups. Tom motioned her toward the couch saying, "Help yourself to some refreshments. You'll have tea, won't you?"

Emma, still bewildered at the situation she found herself, nodded. A thought slid through her head: *Why do I always lose my tongue in stressful situations?* Sitting down in front of the food, she looked from Tom to Bob. Would they tell her why she was here? *Of course they will, you fool! You just have to ask,* she thought to herself. Taking a deep breath, Emma looked from Bob to Tom and finally asked, "Why am I here?"

"We have news about Wolfe," answered Bob.

All the blood drained from Emma's face as her body slumped backwards on the couch. "Is he dead?"

"No," replied Bob and Tom in unison. "He's alive and here in the hospital."

Straightening ready to stand, Emma choked, "I must see him."

"No, no, not until you've eaten, settled into your quarters, and had the situation explained to you."

"Why are you keeping me away from him?" demanded Emma, defiantly standing.

Looking straight at her, Tom, now standing, answered, "Because those are our orders."

Emma returned to the couch, stiff-backed and fuming. Grabbing a sandwich, she shoved it into her mouth as she coldly looked at her jailors. "I've eaten, now show me my quarters."

20

The knock came just as Emma finished hanging up the last of her uniforms. Expecting to see either Tom or Bob, Emma let out a shriek, seeing Juan standing there. "Juan!"

"I'm glad to see you too, kiddo. Ready for good news?"

Hugging him, Emma gestured him to have a seat on the bed. "You had a part in finding Wolfe, didn't you?"

Reaching for her hand, Juan pulled her down beside him. "As a matter of fact, Jesus and I did. That's why I'm here today before you see him."

"Is he so badly injured? I'm a nurse, I've already seen the worst this war hands out. Let's go now," urged Emma, pulling at Juan.

"Yes, you're a very brave and courageous person, Emma, but you need to know what Wolfe has gone through before you visit him."

Resigned, she retook her place beside him, "Okay, tell me and then let me to see him, PLEASE."

"While Wolfe visited at the front," Juan explained, "a German bomb hit the officers' dugout as the trenches were overrun by Germans. Most of the troops and officers were killed during the raid except Wolfe and another officer who was injured. Instead of running for safety, Wolfe stayed behind to tend to the injured officer who died. By the time Wolfe realized he should flee, he discovered his only option was hiding in a one-person trench the size of a coffin used by some British sisters during the early years of the war for safety."

"How awful for him," remarked Emma. "He's afraid of enclosed spaces. Always has been ever since I've known him."

"Yes, and he did a good job of concealing the trench with branches so that the Germans didn't find him, or at least he didn't think so until he heard footstep almost on top of him. He waited and waited, expecting to be shot. But what he heard was a muffled Texas drawl saying, 'Stay put and I'll rescue you.' Every so often he'd hear footsteps approach, stop, and say with the same Texas twang, 'Stay put.'"

Wide eyed, Emma looked at Juan. "What happened? How long was he entombed?"

Jean shook his head. "We don't know. The only story we heard was from a German sergeant named Kurt who saved Wolfe's life."

"Can I see him now?" she asked as she wiped her tear-streaked cheeks with a handkerchief handed her by Juan.

"Yes, but one more thing: he's perpetually in motion. The psychologists say it will pass. But as of now, he doesn't recognize people, not even me."

Wolfe's bed was empty when Emma and Juan walked onto Ward 16. While Juan went searching for a nurse to ask about his whereabouts, Emma walked down the row of beds to see if she recognized any of the patients. Most lay staring up at the ceiling, showing no awareness of their surroundings.

Returning, Juan whispered that Wolfe might be found on the screened porch between Wards 16 and 15. As they walked toward the porch, he said, "The nurse says he spends most of his time out there because he likes the fresh air."

Stepping out onto the porch, Emma stopped abruptly, almost

causing Juan to collide with her. She swallowed the laughter bubbling up. Before her, she saw half a dozen men swaying back and forth in rocking chairs, each to a different drummer. Her eyes sparkled with amusement as she turned to Juan, whispering, "Therapy!"

Nodding, he took hold of her elbow, guiding her down the row of patients until he stopped in front of one frail-looking, gray-haired, hospital-gowned man. "Hello, Wolfe. I've brought you a visitor."

Emma stepped toward Wolfe expecting he'd stop rocking and look up at her, but he continued rocking. He didn't even acknowledge being spoken to. Stooping down in front of the rocker, Emma stopped the chair as she said, "Hello, Wolfe. It's me, Emma. I've come to visit." No response. No eye contact, no change in his face, no sign of recognition, nothing. He reached out, pushed her hand away from the armrest, and began rocking back and forth.

Standing up, Emma turned to Juan. "Does he respond to you? Does he know you?"

Juan shook his head. "No, there's been no recognition of anyone since we returned from the occupied zone. They say he doesn't speak much, but he must hear people because he responds to requests by the nurses and doctors."

"Sounds to me like it's a bad case of shell shock," said Emma as they walked back through the ward heading for the lounge. Juan had made an appointment for Emma to meet with Wolfe's doctor, who made calls during the morning hours when visitors weren't allowed on the ward.

"Many of the soldiers suffer with shell shock," remarked Juan as they walked down the corridor joining the wards. "The closeness of the enemy trenches and the continuous shelling and bombing would rattle anyone, even the horses and mules." After what seemed like miles of halls, they found the doctor's office, a tiny cubbyhole next to the laboratory.

After formal introductions, Emma took the lone chair across from the desk where the doctor sat while Juan stood behind her. "I take it you've come from visiting Captain Gabel?" asked the major, looking at Emma. "Did he recognize you?"

Emma shook her head and glanced down at her lap hiding the disappointment she felt. She couldn't believe her Wolfe wouldn't recognize her.

"Lieutenant Roeder, Emma, may I call you Emma?" Receiving a nod, the doctor continued, "He's been through a terrible experience, worse than many have had to endure. It's going to take time for his mind to deal with hiding in a grave before being taken prisoner. Dealing with the prolonged claustrophobic situation will take time. You must be patient."

Leveling her gaze at the doctor, Emma asked, "And how can I help? I don't have any psychiatric nurses training. I was ordered here to help."

"Yes, Central Command needs your help in bringing Captain Gabel back to health as quickly as possible. First, we need to know the extent the Spanish flu is affecting the German Army. Is it a pandemic? We also need him to vouch for Karl, the German soldier who rescued him."

Emma's mouth formed a large "O" and her eyes widened as she turned toward Juan and extended one hand to him. Stuttering, she managed to say, "I'll ... I'll do my best."

"That's all we ask, Lieutenant Roeder. Your friend here, the captain, has also been assigned to assist. Hopefully, between the two of you, Captain Gabel will recover quickly. Both of you have been given complete access to the patient. I'll continue with his therapy, but if you need anything, let me or the nurse on duty know and we'll see what can be done."

Emma lay wide awake in the comfort of a real bed, the first since her three-day leave to Paris months ago. There were no roommates snoring, coughing, or purring. Only silence of the blackout curtained room. As she turned on her left side after doubling her pillow, her thoughts turned to Wolfe as she'd seen him. Unlike her papa when he'd been in a coma and unable to see her, Wolfe was conscious but unaware of his surroundings. Tears slid down the side of her cheek damping her pillow. This wasn't supposed to happen to them. They'd paid their dues—she lost both her papa and brother, and Wolfe lost his mama. Jabbing her pillow with one hand, she looked upward. "God, why me?"

Expecting no answer, Emma shut her eyes, begging for sleep, but the vision of an inert Wolfe kept sleep at bay. Stretching out on her back, arms thrown over her head with her eyes squinting, "I can find a way, I must," she breathed. "I will not let this defeat us, no way, no how. Have faith, be patient, Wolfe. I will find a way to reach you. The Lord will show me the way. You promised me a wedding and a life of wedded bliss and I'm going to hold you to it."

21

The next morning, Emma found Juan at Wolfe's bedside massaging his legs much as she'd seen Jack Best doing back in Boise with her papa's when they were so hopeful he'd come out of his coma. "Good morning! Getting an early start, I see," she said.

"You bet," responded Juan, bending the leg at the knee. "I hope my therapy annoys him into shouting at me."

Chucking aloud, Emma slapped Juan's shoulder. "If you heal lame horses, you can surely do it with a human."

"No kidding, Emma. Grab that towel there in the hot water, wring it out, and wrap it around Wolfe's other knee so I can work with that one next. Watch out so you don't burn yourself."

"What's that smell?" asked Emma wrinkling her nose.

"Oh, just some liniment-type ointment I concocted. I use it on lame horses," grinned Juan. "Just don't ask me what's in it. It's my miracle for all kinds of ailments, animal or human. Stinky, don't you think?" winked Juan.

Emma wrapped the hot wet towel around Wolfe's knee, looking skeptical. "For humans or animals you say?"

Shrugging, Juan gave her a bemused look as he moved to the other knee. Later that day, as Emma sat with Wolfe on the porch, she considered topics to try to engage his interest. Since she'd arrived at his side, he'd not spoken. "Shell shocked" was the prognosis his doctor gave her, but she wasn't buying it. She'd inherited pigheadedness from two stubborn parents and she wasn't going to give in to a know-nothing diagnoses concocted by battle leery doctors.

"Wolfe, do you remember when we got caught up on top of that barn roof for almost the entire day because a mother boar chased us?"

Was that a slight nod she saw? Emma studied Wolfe. Receiving no answer, not even a change of expression, she looked down at his stockinged feet. Her thoughts went to the first time she'd seen his bare feet. They'd gone wading after one of the drenching rains that that part of Texas sometimes got. They had to remove their shoes and stockings to deliver her loaf of bread, whose yard was flooded all around. Both of them giggled as they each wiggled their freed toes before stepping into the water. It was at that moment she'd noticed how beautiful his feet were. His long slender toes spoke to her for some reason. She was in love from that moment on. Glancing up, Emma thought back over the years about whether she had ever confessed she'd fallen in love with him because of his feet.

No one seemed to know what really happened to him between the time the Germans overran the officer's dugout and when he was found hiding in a basement with a German soldier. Now, back with Allied troops, clean, shaven, and fed, Wolfe either refused to or couldn't talk except for muttering while asleep, "He's my prisoner."

"Nothing makes any sense," remarked Emma as she joined Juan for a cup of coffee in the hospital mess. "What do you think he means when he says, he's my prisoner? Was there anyone around when you found Wolfe?"

"Well, of course there was Kurt, the German soldier who is actually an American citizen from Texas, but no one else."

Emma reached out and gave Juan's hand a pat. "I'm ever so grateful for your searching and finding him."

"I'm just glad Jesus was along and kind of found the basement where they were hiding. I could have missed him if Jesus' good half-Navajo tracking sense hadn't detected them. The two of them could have easily been caught by a German raid or one of ours and killed on sight."

"He was quite far from the hospital where he'd last been sighted?" ventured Emma, fingering her mug.

"Yah, that's what I was told. Strange: where he worked originally was almost a mile away. How did he wander so far without running into British forces, or Germans, for that matter? The distance between trenches, German and British, is minuscule. Only the No-Man's-Land in some areas separates them, but by not much."

"Juan, do you think he'll ever remember what did happen, or will it remain a big fat mystery?"

"I don't know. We'll have to wait and see. Have you finished your coffee? Are you ready to go back?"

Looking up at Juan as they walked back along the hall leading to the porch, Emma winked at her friend. "Thanks for the break."

"Anything for my gal."

22

Emma's temporary assignment to the Paris hospital resulted from the direct intervention of her friend Tom at the American embassy. She was truly fortunate and very appreciative of having such good friends.

Her new quarters, warm and cozy compared to her last assignment where twelve nurses shared a tent, housed four nurses with an inside bathroom and laundry facilities down the hall. It was within walking distance of the mess hall and hospital, with a cobblestone path rather than a muddy one. Emma stored her galoshes out of sight and mind. The only drawback to the assignment was the absence of Thomas the Tom. She missed stroking his soft fur and hearing his snoring at night. Most of all she missed sharing her thoughts and worries with him.

Being low nurse on the roster, she was assigned the night shift, while the other three nurses sharing her quarters worked day shifts. With no female buddy with whom to share even a cup of tea, she felt lonely and isolated for the first time since arriving in France.

As the war continued into 1918, there remained a stalemate on the front on both sides; there'd been no movement, one way or another during the previous year. The Germans had the advantage of dry trenches because they'd been there first and taken the higher ground. The Allied trenches on the whole lay upon flat terrain. The space between the enemy trenches and the Allied trenches was called No-Man's-Land. There wasn't just one trench, but three: a front-line trench, a support trench, and a reserve trench. Troops rotated between the three trenches, with rest periods in the rear trenches or dugouts.

The American troops arriving in late 1917 and early 1918 came with minimum military training, requiring further gunnery practice before being sent to the front to relieve older and battle-weary Allied troops. The chances of these green troops lasting long under constant battle conditions, continuous artillery fire, and close hand-to-hand warfare, was slight. And the longer a soldier experienced the terror of front-line duty, the greater the psychological damage inflicted.

Night duty for Emma entailed calming the reoccurring nightmares of these young patients, for it was while sleeping that they relived their battlefield fears and experiences. They envisioned the Hun coming over into the trench. Their buddies fell beside them, splattering blood over them, their hearts beat double time, and their fingers clutched triggers. They shouted, grunted, and screamed as the nightmare forced them into being victims all over again.

After a night on the wards, Emma emerged mentally and physically worn out from battling these nightmares of her patients. Once she arrived at her quarters, she flung herself on her bed weeping until her well of tears dried up. In a few hours she'd awaken head on a damp pillow and still wearing her nurses uniform. With the sunshine streaming in the windows, she'd change clothes and head for the mess hall, after which she'd make her way to visit Wolfe.

Several weeks passed before Wolfe could stand alone, walk alone, and find his way from the ward to his rocking chair without help. He still remained mute, even though the doctor said there wasn't anything physically wrong. Emma remained hopeful, remembering how she lost her speech during the 1906 earthquake in San Francisco. She regained her speech only after being reunited with her uncle Fritz in New Mexico. She was certain that it would only take time and a significant incident to occur and he'd regain his speech.

Day after day, she sat at his side, talking about mundane and dull topics. Every once in a while, she'd stop, physically turn his face toward her, wink, and say, "Boring you yet with my chitchat that you hate?" Then she'd throw her head back and laugh uproariously before adding, "Say something and I'll stop."

On one visit to the porch, Emma walked along the line of rocking chairs, greeting each patient. Over the past weeks, she'd gotten acquainted with most of them. Despite her lack of interest in card playing, she'd let a few of them teach her how to play poker so she could join in a game with them. On one particular afternoon, she noticed Wolfe observing her as she spoke to the other rocking-chair patients. Was he beginning to notice life taking place around him? After greeting everyone, Emma returned to Wolfe's side, sitting down in her usual chair beside him. Very slowly, Wolfe's hand slid over, grasping hers. She looked over as he bent toward hers. There was recognition in his eyes. His mouth quivered, opened slightly. She saw his tongue through his open lips say, "Emma."

"You spoke!" exclaimed Emma, throwing her arms around him.

One hand clutched her hand, pulling her toward him and into his arms, encircling her tightly as if seeking shelter. "Oh, how I've missed you," she whispered, wrapping him tighter in her arms. They clung together for several minutes before she felt him pull away and returned to rocking.

After first uttering her name and responding with an embrace, he continued his silent rocking but now began making eye contact when she visited. Emma watched as one after another of the rocking-chair patients were discharged and replaced by new faces. She patiently waited for the time Wolfe would be released.

When Emma first arrived at the hospital, she'd attended several lectures for medical staff on the condition called "shell shock," a new battlefield psychosis that resulted in each soldier displaying different symptoms. Some stumbled about with glazed eyes, some with temporary blindness or loss of speech. Most recovered with rest and adequate nourishment, returning to their units. The more severe cases were sent to Hospital 117, located in La Fauche, in the foothills of the Vosges Mountains.

At one of these lectures, Emma met Dr. Thomas W. Salmon, who advocated a program of work along with rest and good food for the more seriously affected patients and referred to them as having NYD, meaning "not yet diagnosed." "We Americans didn't like using the term shell shocked," he explained, because of the varying psychological conditions exhibited, "so we use an acronym." During her conversation with Dr. Salmon, he suggested she interest Wolfe in assisting patients, starting perhaps by taking him with her on her duty shift. With the help of Dr. Salmon, Emma began working day shifts with Wolfe shadowing her as she working on the wards.

One day as Emma sat with Wolfe holding his hand, he began telling her what he could remember about his capture.

He'd gone up to the British aid station at the invitation of one of the officers. It had been quiet on the front, with little or no trench warfare. This wasn't unusual because, by a "gentleman's agreement," many times, both sides took a breather from fighting to give the troops a rest from the constant fear of frontal attack.

Eager to visit his British friend, he hitched a ride with a supply wagon going up to the front. Once there, he not only took care of his friend's medical problem but checked on some of the enlisted men who were having trouble with their feet or old wounds.

At the invitation of his friend, he remained for supper with the officers in their dugout several yards from the main trench, which was uniquely British because it zig-zagged rather than being straight like the American's trenches. During their meal, the Germans rushed the British trenches, surprising the soldiers and inflicting heavy casualties.

While attending to the wounded, a German soldier entered the dugout where Wolfe was. The Hun, using sign language, insisted he follow him and leave his patient. "I tried to argue with him, but to no avail, and he was surprised at my speaking German. Being unarmed and with a gun pointed directly at me, I complied," said Wolfe.

"Upon leaving the dugout, the German indicated I was to crotch down and run away from No-Man's-Land rather than head toward the enemies' side. It didn't make any sense. He pushed me into a small one-man trench often used by British nurses, covering me with branches and dirt, ordering in English, 'Stay quiet. I'll be back to get you.'"

Looking up at Emma, Wolfe shivered. "I waited all doubled up in that tiny earthlike coffin listening to running feet, gunfire, and Germans' shouting. I don't know why they didn't find me or at least fall into the small bunker where I hid. I prayed. I tried to figure out why an English-speaking German soldier would hide me rather than shooting me or taking me prisoner. Nothing made sense. As it got colder, I began to shake, my teeth chattered, and I wanted to sleep but I knew I had to stay awake if I was to survive. Pretty soon, silence prevailed except the pounding of heavy rain. It beat on the leaves covering my grave and the mud dripped through onto me with revenge. My throat was dry but I couldn't catch enough rain drops with my tongue to satisfy my thirst. I was just about to poke my head up through the branches covering me when a rat scampered across my chest, making me jerk out of the branches above.

"'I thought I told you to stay hidden,' barked the German soldier who'd captured me, pointing his gun at me. I grunted and replied, 'You'd jump out of your skin too if a big fat rat ran across your chest.' He just looked at me and pointed in the direction he wanted me to walk. For the next few days, I was locked in a windowless basement closet of sorts. Sometimes, my captor looked in on me but most of the time he left me alone listening to the constant artillery and gunfire. I wanted to escape but felt so disoriented and fearful that I couldn't find the courage. One time I did break free and tried to make my way to the trees a distance from the house but he caught me. It was then that he finally explained he wanted to escape from the German Army and return home to America. He'd come over to Germany to visit family in 1916. When the U.S. joined the Allies, he'd been conscripted into the Army before he could leave the country. He'd been waiting for an opportunity to give himself up without being shot. He thought finding me gave him that opportunity.

"As he talked, I wondered how he planned to make this happen without us both being shot as deserters or, worse yet, as spies, since both of us were Americans who spoke German. Our discussion was interrupted by sniper fire around the outside of the house. As the sound of heavy boots came through the door, my German captor arose, quickly pointing his gun at me.

"In German he shouted, 'On your feet, prisoner!' Startled, I stood up with my hands raised. The men who entered the house carried a wounded soldier. They lowered him to the floor as my captor said, 'My prisoner's a doctor. Let him help.'

"For the next few hours, as the battle raged around us, German patients started arriving but, with no supplies or my bag, I could do little to help except bind up the wounds of the living with strips of cloth from the dead. As daylight faded, a heavy smoke hung around the house, and the sounds of battle ceased, as well as the tide of patients. I finally slumped to the floor exhausted, thankful I was still alive. My German captor handed me a mug of cold coffee, a hunk of cheese, and a scrap of bread.

"I awoke to complete silence and, shifting my stiff body, I glanced around, where I saw sleeping men whose snores and labored breathing replaced the groans of the wounded. As I struggled to sit up, I felt a hand clutch my arm, pinning me down. Beside me was my German soldier, his young face dark with the beginnings of whiskers, his bright blue eyes tense and alert.

"Drawing close, he whispered in my ear, 'What part of Texas are you from?'

"Turning, I murmured, 'The Hill Country, New Braunfels.'

"'Aw, that explains why you speak German fluently.'

"Nodding, I asked, 'And you?'

"'Houston,' he muttered, slouching back against the wall as his right hand stroked his chin. 'Boy, could I do with a bath, a shave and a warm meal.'

"Looking over at his mud-caked uniform, I sympathized with him as I looked at my own dirt-encrusted clothing. My boots, once shiny enough to pass inspection even in a wartime operating room, now were encrusted with yellowish mud mixed with slime. I eyed my captor beside me who appeared to have dropped back to sleep along with everyone else. I shifted my position thinking to escape.

"'Don't even try it without me,' came a tight-lipped command beside me. 'We get out of here together or not at all.'

"Settling my stiff body back into a less painful position, I glanced over at my German soldier, for he had become my German during the last hours. 'What do you mean, together?'

"'I mean just that,' he said. 'You're going to be my ticket out of this mess I'm in.' I looked over at the speaker and made a face. 'No, no, we're going to do this together so both of us don't get shot. I've thought it all through. As we head toward the Allied line, when we meet Germans, you will be my prisoner, but when we meet Americans or Frenchmen, I will become your prisoner. Got it?'

"'Yaw, I get the plan,' I said. 'We'll end up both being shot as traitors.'

"'Not if we're careful, we won't. We have one gun between us that we can use as the situation demands.'

"'Why do you want to do this? Why do you think I want to do this?'

"The young German opened his eyes, 'I never intended to get caught up in this war. All I wanted was to visit my German family before I started college and look where it got me. I just want to go back to Texas to my family.'

"I reached out, placing my hand on my captor's knee, giving it a squeeze. 'Okay, we'll try, but it's your move first. You have to get me, or should I say us, out of this house and headed toward the Allied lines. I haven't got the faintest idea of where I'm at.'"

Emma watched as Wolfe stopped speaking, head bowed. She reached across, giving him a hug that brought a weak smile.

Rocking back in his chair, he said almost in a whisper, "I was scared, still not totally trusting this German who held my life in his hands. But what choice did I have?"

23

Taking a deep breath, Wolfe took Emma's hand in his, brought it to his lips to give it a kiss before continuing his story. "I ran hunched over following my captor. It took until we were safely away from the house before he revealed his name was Kurt, explaining if I used his name in front of other Germans, there would be suspicion that something was up between us.

"Keeping up with him was difficult because of all the bomb craters, splintered trees, and human litter. Besides that, I wasn't in any physical condition to run for any length of time dodging and jumping around impediments. Suddenly, Karl stopped and ran behind me. I felt the barrel of a gun touch my back. I heard footsteps coming toward us. They were speaking German.

"'Auch, you've caught one of them,' said one of the advancing German soldiers.

"I stood shaking with hands on top of my head; my legs felt like jelly. In my head I kept telling myself not to faint.

"'Guten arbeit!' grunted one of the Germans. 'Do you want us to walk along with you as you take him in?'

"At this point I gained enough control that I noticed a look pass between the soldiers. They suspected something about Karl and me. So I wasn't surprised when they suggested we go along with them, especially when they pointed out that we were moving in the direction of the Allied lines rather than toward the German line. As we retraced our steps, I wondered how we were going to get out of this predicament. While stepping into a clearing, the sound of an airplane overhead was heard. Instinctively, everyone hit the ground as bullets cascaded around us. The plane banked and returned, showering us with another round of bullets Finally, the plane's engine grew fainter. The danger was past.

"Raising my head, I checked on Karl. He was safe, but what of the others? Slowly, Karl and I searched the other soldiers. Scattered among them, we saw Germans bloodied and withering in pain. Some were dead. I went from one to the other of the wounded, checking on their condition. I told Karl there wasn't much I could do for them without bandages and medicine. Too bad the Germans don't carry emergency medical supplies with them like the Americans.

"Karl urged me to leave the wounded soldiers but tagged along as I checked the condition of each man. Kneeling down beside one of the Germans, I placed his hand on his chest. Pulling his coat tight around the wound, I tried to stop the bleeding. Removing the man's belt, I wrapped it around his chest to hold the jacket tight.

"Speaking in German, I said, 'That's about all I can do for you,' as I glanced into the man's blue frightened eyes before following Karl back toward the French line. *He could have been a relative*, I thought. 'May God help you,' I whispered."

Emma watched as Wolfe slumped back in the rocking chair, hands clenching the chair arms. He'd withdrawn from the world, including her. Patting his arm as she rose, she quietly said, "Rest. I'm going for tea and biscuits for us. It's long past the time for refreshments." After a silent partaking of the scones with jelly and clotted cream along with several cups of tea, Wolfe seemed ready to continue telling his story.

"As the sun set, Karl and I stumbled into an abandoned German trench near No-Man's-Land. High on a hill overlooking the enemy line, the wind swept down upon us permeating our woolen uniforms, freezing our faces and hands. A search of the trench yielded no bodies, no extra clothing, or food. We'd consumed all the rations we'd pilfered. Between us we had only a few mouthfuls of water left.

"'Pray that there's no moon tonight,' said Karl, 'or we'll be sitting targets for your planes.'

"'Mumm,' I muttered, not feeling much like talking. I was freezing and had never known such hunger. The grip in my middle told me my body was now eating at the lining of my stomach. Moving my tongue around my mouth, I tried to create saliva to take my desire to drink the last swallow of water left. This was going to be another long tortuous night.

"As darkness blanketed the trench, both of us attempted to identify every sound we heard, fearful of attack but worried about the unusual silence. Suddenly, leaning close to me, Karl asked, 'Do you hear … ' His question was cut short as we were set upon by two forms. Karl's gun landed in front of me. As I turned toward him, a hand suddenly slid across my mouth. 'Shush—you're okay. We're Americans.'

"Shaking my head in an effort to speak, I struggled, but still recognized the voice: Juan! After I stopped struggling, the hand was removed. 'What the Sam hill?!'

"'Jesus and I are here to rescue you. We've been tracking you for several days. Let's get you over to the Allied lines.'

"'What have you done to Karl?' I asked, crawling toward his prone body. Reaching him, I turned him over, feeling the wetness on his shoulder. They'd stabbed him. 'You idiots,' I cried, 'He's American!'

"'He's German,' cursed Juan.

"I began putting pressure on Karl's wound to stop the bleeding. 'Give me your knapsack,' I ordered, grabbing the small package of medical supplies from Juan. I bound the wound tightly. 'It's all right Karl, these are friends. They'll get us across to the Allied side. I'll fix you up as good as new once we're safe.'"

Wolfe lapsed into silence. Emma noticed his hands grappling with the front of his hospital gown, apparently reliving the stress at trying to save his friend's life. Instinctively she reached out, grasping his hand and drawing close. Wolfe turned toward her, pulling her close. "It's so wonderful having you close. You smell so sweet."

24

Before Wolfe continued telling his story, Emma enticed him into a walk down the length of the porch. Going slowly arm in arm, they stopped in front of each rocker to greet the occupant. Not all responded but most returned their greetings with nods or smiles. With the stiffness gone from her legs from sitting so long, Emma was ready to take her chair beside Wolfe as he took up his story where he'd left off.

"The artillery shelling kept all of us hunkered down in the basement of a bombed-out house adjunct to No-Man's-Land on the German side. It was an incredible place to hide. Jesus had located it when he scoured our surroundings for a warm place to hide rather than the open trench on the hill. Abandoned by the Germans, it provided real beds, food, an indoor latrine, running water, and electric lights!

"Karl laughed at us as we marveled at the luxury of the digs. Nothing like it existed on the Allied side, where the troops, even the officers, endured mud-filled dugouts—let alone real beds! To amuse his newfound countrymen, Karl described German dugouts he'd visited that were better than the one we were presently inhabiting. 'Some have their own ventilation systems, wallpapered front rooms, painted ceiling, telephones, real beds, and perhaps even paneled walls.'

"As we waited out the shelling, we indulged in the stored food in the abandoned house, made coffee, and talked about how much better off the Germans seemed to be. 'No wonder it looked like they were winning the war,' commented Juan. He'd heard the shipment of food supplies across the English Channel had been hampered by the German U-boats, but now that had ceased since America had entered the war. Food flowed freely between England and France."

"The shelling never stopped?" Emma asked.

Brushing his fingers over his hair, he answered, "No, and sitting about under constant fire was a relatively new experience for Juan. Normally, his days were filled with exercising injured horses or mules and readying them for return to duty. However, that had changed when he'd learned of my disappearance and probable capture by the Germans. General Pershing had granted him permission along with Jesus, a sergeant under Juan's command, to go on a search and rescue mission to find me."

Wolfe explained to Emma that Juan chose Jesus as his companion because the Navajo was an expert code breaker and tracker, as well as a close friend from New Mexico. Jesus grew up on the Indian reservation bordering the lands owned by Juan's family. The two had gone to school together, played hooky together, and hunted and fished together over the course of their childhood. Although Wolfe hadn't known Jesus until his arrival in Santa Fe, they became friends through Juan, enjoying many forays into the mountains hunting.

Wolfe mentioned that Juan didn't entirely trust Karl even after he vouched for him, saying, "He never let him out of his sight." His story of having been compelled to join the German Army while visiting relatives sounded fabricated. With all the German loyalist he'd heard about back in Texas in the early days of the war, skepticism remained. Wolfe admitted to Emma that Juan had every reason to doubt Karl's loyalty too. He himself also had been suspicious in the beginning, wondering if he'd gotten tired of soldiering and decided a way out was latching onto an American captive like Wolfe. Would he switch his allegiance again if faced by other German soldiers?

Recalling that while checking Karl's wound, he noticed Juan signaled Jesus to slip through the tunnel leading outside, probably for reconnaissance. Not being a military man, just a physician, he realized that the sound of battle had suddenly gone silent, signaling something might be up. Wolfe said he saw Juan take a defense position near the tunnel's entrance, listening intently for any indication that Jesus had met resistance. Apparently hearing nothing, Juan slid to a kneeling position, gun cocked, ready to halt a small group if an attempted entrance occurred, realizing a large number could easily overpower him.

"The hair on the back of my neck itched, warning me that we were in danger and in need of a second escape route. Surely, the Germans had thought about that. Glancing around our cramped space, I looked for one. Initially, they'd been so delighted to have found somewhere to get out of the artillery fire, none of them had viewed the space properly except for the necessities, primarily warmth and safety.

"Shortly, I noticed Juan skirting the perimeter of the basement scrutinizing every inch of the space. There were several wooden chests stacked against the walls but when he moved them, he found nothing. He stood in the middle of the room, slowly turning around, surveying every inch of the room again. 'There has to be an exit,' he muttered. Squatting down in front of me, Juan whispered, 'I've checked the most logical places for another exit with no luck. Where would the Germans hide a second exit?'

"I tensed at Juan's question, realizing the importance of it. Slowly, I began to dissect the space around us like I would a human body on a gurney. As my eyes traveled over the walls of the cellar, I recalled Paw telling that most homes in the old country didn't have basements, but this was a French farm house in the wine country, not German, so maybe it would have something … Oh, wait a minute, now that I thought about it, some smaller French farm houses had wine cellars or hollowed out spaces where they kept bottled wine to age, usually in tiny earthen holes the size for one bottle. With the war, I bet the farmer probably covered over its entrance. 'I have an idea!' I said to Juan as I stood and walked slowly around the room examining the walls from ceiling to floor.

"'What are you looking for?' asked Juan, 'Can I help?'

"I signaled for silence as I studied the floor at my feet next to the wall. I pushed against the paneling. A space no more than seventeen inches wide and three feet high, just barely enough for someone to slip through, appeared. Grinning, I turned to Juan. 'There it is. Want to explore?'

"It didn't take another invitation for Juan to slither through the opening. Shining his flashlight ahead of him, he crawled around until at one end of the narrow trench, he came upon what he'd hoped to find: a rock leaning against the outside wall. Sliding the rock to one side, he poked his head out. He was between two rows of grapevines next to the farmer's chicken coop. Satisfied with his find, Juan retraced his path, reentering the basement. 'Well, we have a second escape route,' announced Juan, just as Jesus burst in and the artillery on both sides began again. They could be hit directly or indirectly by either side. Our fate, all four of us, was in the hands of God."

"Emma, I need water," Wolfe said suddenly. "I'm parched."

Reaching for the water pitcher on the table beside her, Emma said, "I've got to go fetch some fresh water. It won't take but a minute."

Taking gulps of water from the glass offered, Wolfe gave Emma a contented look as he handed her the empty glass. "Boy, what I would have given while in captivity and on the run for a glass of water like that. Water from a canteen always tastes brackish," he said, smacking his lips together in a boyish way to show satisfaction.

25

Rejuvenated by the taste of the sweet local water Emma had provided, Wolfe settled back in his rocking chair ready to continue his story. Pausing, he smiled broadly as he gave her hand a pat before withdrawing it to clasp the arm of the rocker. Glancing toward the adjoining building, he gritted his teeth before returning his gaze to his betrothed.

"Despite his injury, Karl urged us to escape. 'Go, go. I'll delay them as much as possible,' he said, waving Juan and I through the wine cellar dugout. He quickly adjusted his sling over his arm and strode back to where he'd been seated, when we'd heard the ruckus of jovial German voices. Later Karl revealed he'd hurriedly hidden our empty mugs left on the table. Facing the entering soldiers, he prayed we'd make it through to the vineyard safely and that we could intercept Jesus before he tried to enter the hideout.

"Karl told us afterward that three laughing soldiers burst into the house, shoving each other like children playing a game. At the sight of him, they stopped, looking like the teenagers caught playing hooky from school. Startled at seeing him, they made no move to raise their rifles at Karl but drew closer to one another as if for protection. Karl said he rose to his full height, towering over all three by more than a foot, asking sternly, 'What have we here, deserters? Where are you supposed to be?'

"All three suddenly stood at attention in front of him. The oldest of the three sputtered, 'Sir, we got lost as we came back across

No-Man's-Land. This was the first German outpost we stumbled upon, Sir.'

"Karl said he remained as authoritarian as he could, asking, 'What unit are you with that you've strayed this far south? There hasn't been fighting in this area for at least a week except for my group that's out scouting around. I'm surprised you didn't run into them.'

"As the young soldiers looked from one to the other, Karl remained as serious as he could, pointed to the rifles the men held lackadaisically at their sides, and said, 'If you'd faced the enemy when you entered here, you'd all be dead. Don't you know how to use your armament?'

"Mortified, all three blond heads bowed as the oldest replied, 'None of us have any bullets, Sir.'

"Karl said he swallowed a laugh. He wondered what had happened to the old strict Prussian military code he'd heard so much about from his German father, who himself had served in the Prussian Army prior to immigrating to Texas in 1850. Looking at the weary young men in front of him, he then invited them to help themselves to water and whatever food they could find. 'Rest easy, men,' he directed. 'I'm going out for a look around and then I'll be back.' And with that, he grabbed his rifle and escaped."

"After Karl rejoined us," said Wolfe, "it was decided that he should abandon most of his German uniform and wear a few pieces of clothing donated by Jesus since they were approaching a section of No-Man's-Land where it was considered safe to cross over into Allied territory.

"As they waited on the edge of No-Man's-Land for the sun to set, we huddled in a dry trench on the side of a hill overlooking a quiet section of the French countryside. Across the savaged ground between the two armies, we looked down on the Allied trenches, observing movement but no gunfire. Here and there beyond the front trenches were other dugouts, probably for officers or used as rest areas for battle-weary soldiers. As Juan surveyed the landscape, he shook his head in disgust. 'No wonder this war has gone on so long. The Allied Army has the low ground, a definite advantage to the enemy on the higher hills where everything can be observed.'

"Under his breath, Jesus agreed. 'Why do you suppose we Navajos won so many battles on the American frontier? We used the high ground to our advantage.' As we waited for nightfall, each in deep thought except Jesus who, hawk-like, kept his jet-black eyes peeled on the landscape.

"We crossed No-Man's-Land without incident thanks to the Navajo's shrewd guidance. Being reunited with French and British troops assigned the section of the battle line meant being transported to the nearest Allied headquarters for repatriation. On my insistence Kurt received immediate medical treatment." Wolfe chuckled as he told Emma, "Before climbing into the ambulance, Juan checked the horse's hooves for rot, a condition most suffered from because of the muddy roads; furthermore, he told the driver, 'Both horses' hooves require care. See to it.' As the wagon rumbled away from the front lines, all of us slumped on the hard flooring allowing pent-up stress and weariness to take over."

Turning to Emma, who had sat on the edge of her chair all through Wolfe's telling of his experiences behind enemy lines, Wolfe drew her close to him saying, "I was so scared I'd never see you again. Wanting to be with you kept me going. I felt God's and your spirit with me, urging me to survive." Arms around each other, they kissed, unaware of the other patients around them.

After a long embrace, both Wolfe and Emma drew apart. Her face flushed, Emma took a quick look around. No one seemed to have noticed their behavior. She turned to Wolfe, who had returned to rocking, lost in his ruminations.

26

"Wolfe," Emma said quietly. Receiving no answer, she rose from her chair, walked to the stand at the screen window to aimlessly scrutinize the building across the way. Its paint was peeling, the windows dirty, and the roof sagged. Between the two buildings, the weeds stood knee high. Like the shell-shocked patients on the porch behind her, both the building and the men suffered from the conflict of mankind. She turned back toward Wolfe, rocking, unaware of her but back in a world of his own.

In a trance, Emma found herself leaving the building and hurrying toward a grassy space across from the hospital. Searching for happy memories to boost her morale, she passed wheelchair patients pushed by nuns, men struggling with crutches, and napping men on benches with eyes closed and chins resting on chests. Suddenly, she heard her name being called. Turning toward the voice, she watched as she saw a nurse waving.

"Oh, thanks for waiting for me. I was afraid I'd never catch up with you," said Maddie.

"Maddie, what are you doing here?!" exclaimed Emma, throwing her arms around her friend. "I didn't know you were stationed here at the base hospital."

"I'm not. I'm here to visit my brother, Kurt. You remember my telling you about him, don't you?"

"Yes, of course I remember. He's been rescued! I hope his wounds are healing well."

"How did you know he'd been injured?"

"Come and I'll tell you," said Emma, motioning Maddie toward a bench. "I'm ready for some girl time right now. I heard that your brother saved an American doctor who in turn helped him to escape."

Maddie, bubbling over with excitement, sat beside Emma ready to share her good news. "Oh, Emma, Kurt was so fortunate during the last raid he was on; he kept an American doctor from capture …"

"Yes, Maddie—could that doctor's name be Wolfe?" interrupted Emma, beaming from ear to ear.

"Why yes, how did you know?"

"Because Wolfe is my fiancé. He's just returned from being held by a German soldier, an American who deserted from the German Army."

Both Maddie's hands flew up to her mouth as she covered a squeal. "No way! I'll be darned!"

"Yep! One and the same," said Emma, smiling as she reached for Maddie. The two girls wrapped their arms around each other, swaying in joy. As their elation decreased, Emma asked, "How's your brother doing? Is his shoulder healing?"

Maddie pulled out a handkerchief and dabbed her eyes before answering. "Oh, he's doing great now that they have the gangrene taken care of. Your Wolfe did a wonderful job of caring for him without any medication after removing the bullet. I will always be so grateful. How is Wolfe? I heard he's here in the hospital. Is he sick?"

Emma glanced downward before answering. "He's suffering from shell shock of the worst sort. He mostly rocks and stares into space."

Moving closer to Emma, Maddie embraced her, saying, "Oh, no! How terrible!"

Nodding, Emma melted into the comforting arms of her fellow

Texan. For a while, she lost herself in the joy of consoling nearness of another human being before she sat back and looked into the sympathetic eyes of her friend.

Taking hold of Emma's hand, Maddie asked, "Do you think I could visit him? I want to thank him for helping Kurt escape, as well as taking such good care of him after he was shot."

"I think he'd like that, "answered Emma, "but I don't know if you'll get much of a response from him."

"Well, I want to meet him. I'm so grateful that he has given me my brother back. I don't know what I would have done if I'd lost Kurt. He's not only my brother but my best friend, who keeps me grounded. We weren't always close," she chuckled, "but after our teen years, we started doing things together while on visits home from college. Most of our former friends had married early, had families, or other interest than ours, so I guess it was only natural that we teamed up during those times we were home. I've missed him so," she confided.

"How did Maddie's visit with Wolfe go?" asked Juan, taking a seat across from Emma at the hospital mess hall.

"Great, I guess," responded Emma placing her silverware around her plate after unwrapping it from her napkin. "He stopped rocking when I introduced her and even looked straight up at her. She sat in the chair beside his rocker and explained who she was and how grateful she felt for saving Kurt. As she talked, he looked around at the other men rocking, something he doesn't do when I visit."

"Did he talk to her?" asked Juan.

"No, he just listened. She sat there for over an hour chatting about their childhood back in Houston. I was surprised at how long she stayed. A couple of times she patted his hand, which seemed strange to me, but everyone has their own way of expressing thankfulness, I guess."

"You weren't feeling a little jealous?" asked Juan, giving her his special twinkling eye.

"No, no, of course not. She was just showing friendship," replied Emma through clenched teeth. "Let's change the subject."

"Sure. What do you want to talk about? The weather?"

Throwing the *Army News* at him that she'd been reading, she looked at her plate to shove a few bites around while settling her thoughts. Yes, she had to admit, she had been jealous, but Juan didn't have to say it. Just then, she felt her shoe kicked. Looking up, she encountered a smiling Juan shoveling his squash into his mouth while planning a frontal attack under the table. *Well, two can play at this game*, thought Emma, reaching under the table to untie her shoe lace. Then, she carefully took her foot out of her shoe and with her toes inched up under his pant leg. Under her eyelashes, she watched him try to control the tickling he was experiencing. *No one has ticklish legs like Juan*, smiled Emma to herself.

"Stop it, Emma!" he blurted out, "Or, I'll …"

"You'll what?"

27

By chance, Emma decided to visit Kurt's ward to see how his shoulder was healing. She found Wolfe bent over Kurt with Maddie at his side ready to assist. She turned to leave before being seen. *When did Wolfe start visiting patients,* she wondered, *and why didn't he tell me? Had Maddie somehow persuaded him to visit her brother? She knew that Maddie was visiting Wolfe on a regular basis.* Jealous that his first outing away from his own ward wasn't with her, Emma hurried from the ward.

Returning to her quarters, Emma threw herself onto her bed, chastising herself for not confronting the two when she'd seen them together. She'd known that Maddie had been visiting Wolfe but she didn't know just how frequently. She herself had visited less often recently because her nursing duties had doubled now that the Americans were pushing the German troops back. Rumor had it that the Spanish flu had cost them dearly; a major intended attack had even been called off because of it.

Even Juan and Jesus had been ordered out on another secret rescue mission behind the German lines. She hadn't seen either one of them for at least a week so she'd had no one to talk to about her nagging concerns about Wolfe's recovery. How she missed Juan.

Reaching under her pillow, she pulled out her picture of Wolfe taken while he attended medical school in Denver. He looked so youthful and content, pleased with himself at graduation and her saying "yes" to his marriage proposal. They'd known for years they loved each other. The two of them had even made plans for marriage after his internship and her receiving her nursing certificate. But then the war got in the way, making them postpone their plans. Now it appeared that might not happen at all. She had competition: Maddie. She still loved him but she was confused by his behavior during the last few weeks, and now this. Did he still love her? Emma pressed the framed picture to her chest and closed her eyes.

The sound of voices entering the barracks roused Emma from a deep sleep. Befuddled, she couldn't figure out where she was but then the weight of something pressing on her chest jogged her memory. Slipping the picture back under her pillow, she lay back, allowing her grogginess to slip into awareness. Throwing her feet over the side of the cot and fighting the desire to go back to sleep, she shoved her feet into her shoes, pulled herself up off the bed, and headed to the lavatory.

"Emma, are you in here?" she heard someone call. "Someone wanted to see you. Says it's urgent."

"I'll be there in just a moment," hollered Emma from a commode stall. Washing and drying her hands, Emma emerged to find the barracks empty. "Hum, wonder what happened to my uninvited guest?" said Emma aloud. Grabbing her jacket, she walked out the door, bumping into Juan sitting on the stoop.

"Whoa, there. Don't be in such a hurry."

"Sorry, you're back! What's so urgent?"

Juan grinned at her as he held out a hand. "Come with me, I have a surprise for you."

Emma let Juan grab her hand as he led her toward the hospital. "Where are we going?"

"You'll see, just have patience. It's a surprise, one that's going to blow your boots off if you have any on," teased Juan glancing down as he gave her hand two squeezes.

Juan slowed, checking on the ward numbers as Emma realized they'd come to the wards where the serious surgical patients resided. Why would a surprise be in this section of the hospital? Who could he be dragging her to see? Suddenly, he stopped and held the door open for her.

With a wave of his hand, he invited her ahead of him. As she stepped along, she looked at the people's faces hoping her surprise wasn't a former patient. Some of the men sat propped up, others lay flat on their backs with arms bent under their heads giving them height to look around. As she neared the middle of the ward, she turned with a questioning look at Juan but he waved her on. Suddenly, her eye caught sight of a patient in a prone position with something brownish clutched beside him. Emma slowed, vision glued to the person on the bed. Then she recognized what he was holding. A violin! She held her breath as she focused on the patient's face. "Edmund?" She sobbed, dropping to her knees beside the bed. "Is it really you?"

"Yes, it's me," choked Edmund, reaching out to clasp her with his unbandaged hand.

Bewildered, Emma allowed Juan to assist her into a chair next to the bed. Glancing first at her long-lost brother and then up at Juan, she asked, "How did you find him?" Turning to Edmund, she whispered, "Where have you been all these years? We've searched everywhere for you!"

Bringing his violin across his body to cradle it in his bandaged arm and against his chest, Edmund adjusted his position so he faced his sister. "I have a long story to tell you. Do you have time now?"

28

Emma lay on her bed pondering the tale her brother had chronicled. Edmund's memory was blank concerning how he ended up being cared for by a kind woman after the San Francisco earthquake. In the beginning, he thought she was a nurse, but then he realized he wasn't in a hospital but a private home. As time passed, he recalled going into a building to find someone but he couldn't remember who because something hit him, knocking him out. When he awoke, he was at the home of Mrs. Scott, who'd opened up her house to the injured during the earthquake.

After regaining his strength, he'd gone searching for the family he suspected he had. Since his last memory was of visiting a ship, Edmund said he went to the harbor in hopes he'd discover his identity by talking to the captain of the ship he visited. Unfortunately, the ship had left port. Returning to Mrs. Scott's, he began helping her care for people who required a place to stay while they healed from injuries received care during and after the earthquake.

As the number of wounded from the quake dwindled, a need for housing, created by the destruction of the earthquake, arose. Since Mrs. Scott had lost her husband, she had no means of support other than her home. She decided to open a boardinghouse with Edmund's help. The two of them managed to earn enough to live on. He continued searching for his family, with little success because of not knowing his last name, but he never gave up hope.

A year after the earthquake, a pianist rented one of their rooms while he played at a tavern in the city. One day a fellow musician, a violinist, visited, so the two could practice together in the hopes of forming a duo. As Edmund listened to them practice, he said he was attracted by the music, especially the violin. When the two went into lunch, the violin was left out of its case. Edmund picked it up and, to his surprise, his fingers automatically knew their placement on the strings and his right hand knew how to handle the bow. Soon he became aware of an audience.

"Where did you learn to play like that, boy?" asked Mrs. Scott's roomer.

As he replaced the violin in its case, Edmund shook his head, saying, "I don't know. I didn't know I could play."

"Well, you've received very professional training, that's for sure."

Edmund looked at the speaker, dumbfounded. And then he saw a woman's face in front of him. Shaking his head to see the image better, he answered, "Mother was a pianist and I took up the violin." Puzzled at his own answer, he turned to Mrs. Scott. "Is that possible?"

Using the edge of the sheet, Emma wiped away a tear as she recalled her brother telling of the return of his musical ability. He had always been the naturally talented one in the family, even more so than Mama or Papa, who both played the violin. How extraordinary that three of her family—Mama, Papa, and Edmund—suffered memory loss because of the earthquake.

Sleep overtook Emma until a few hours later when she awoke with a start, thinking of Edmund's telling of the years he'd toured many small towns in the West with his musician friends, living from hand to mouth on their meager earnings, playing in taverns and sometimes giving musical concerts for citizens at small-town theaters. Emma wondered how she might have felt if she'd lived such a nomadic life during her teen years rather than finishing her education, working with her papa at the mercantile, and continuing her violin practicing. Shaking her head as she dressed for the day, Emma couldn't imagine struggling as Edmund did. Thank goodness she'd been able to return to her family, even though it had been rough at times.

Distracted with the knowledge that she'd found her brother, Emma visited Wolfe, whom she found intent on his rocking, but he stopped the moment she entered the porch. "I hear you've found your brother."

Surprised at his attention, she sat next to him. "Yes, Juan found him and was able to bring him here to the base hospital. He might lose his arm, his left one. It would break his heart."

"Do you want me to have a look and see what I think?"

"Are you up to seeing a patient?" asked Emma, puzzled by Wolfe's apparent interest.

Getting up from the rocker, Wolfe held out an arm to her. "Let's go and have a look at your brother's arm."

Clad in his hospital dressing gown, Wolfe walked purposefully toward the bed on which Edmund lay. Unsmiling, he said, "Hello, Edmund. I'm Wolfe, your sister's friend. I've come to take a look at your arm. Emma, please unwrap it."

Mindful of a ward nurse approaching at top speed, Emma glanced at Wolfe before beginning to do as he'd asked. She didn't miss that he was checking on her brother's lungs and heart rate.

"What do you think you're doing?" asked the ward nurse, whom Emma didn't recognize.

Wolfe glanced up as the nurse stopped at the foot of Edmund's bed. "I'm going to take a look at this patient's arm."

"You can't do that," replied ward nurse. "You're not a doctor.

Only a doctor is allowed … You are a patient. Get back to your ward this instant."

Raising his hand to the nurse, Wolfe said, "Stop telling me what I can and can't do. I see this patient is scheduled for surgery today."

"Yes, we're ready to send him to surgery for the arm to be amputated. Now stop what you're doing."

Turning his back on the ward nurse, Wolfe bent over the bed and began examining the injured hand and arm. "Mumm, can you feel this?" he asked Edmund as he put pressure on various parts of the wrist and fingers. "Move the fingers for me. Yes, that's good," said Wolfe as he watched the fingers jerk.

"Yes, I can feel it," answered Edmund tight lipped, as Wolfe continued to probe upward on the arm.

Straightening up to his full height, Wolfe turned to Emma. "I'm certain I can save this arm and repair the damage to the hand." Turning to the ward nurse he said, "You said the operating room was ready for this patient now?"

Fuming and tight lipped the nurse snorted, "Yes, but not for your use," smartly turning around and marching toward the end of the ward.

"Emma, I'll stay here with Edmund while you go find, ah—" he said, flipping through the chart, "Captain Leeds for me and see if he'd be so kind as to come here to see me."

As Emma raced off, Wolfe sat on the edge of the bed, holding out his hand to Edmund's good hand saying, "Glad to meet you. I've heard about you while your sister was staying with your father's family in Texas. We had great fun hunting armadillos, fishing, and getting into lots of trouble. Well, she got into trouble and I did the rescuing."

Edmund smiled and nodded. "I rescued her many times too. I know how that goes with her. Guess you're planning to do that on a permanent basis."

Getting up as he saw Emma returning with Captain Leeds, Wolfe grinned. "Hope so," he said as he moved to intercept his colleague before he reached Edmund's bed.

Emma's smug smile alerted Wolfe that she was up to something as she slipped her hand through the captain's arm beside her. "Wolfe, let me introduce you to my good friend, Captain Leeds, who I served with when I first arrived in France." Turning toward the captain, she said, "This is my fiancé, Wolfe, who you've heard me mention." As the two doctors greeted each other, Emma left them and headed toward her brother's bedside, saying over her shoulder, "I'll leave you two to talk."

Edmund looked up as she approached, still dizzy at his good luck at having been found by Juan and thereby reunited with his long-lost sister, whose fiancé, a doctor, might be able to save his arm, which meant so much to him.

Beside the bed, Emma clasped Edmund's good hand in hers. "You're going to have the best team ever working on saving your arm and hand. I know the surgery will be a success." As the two doctors approached, she gave his hand a squeeze, winked, and rose to give them room to examine the injury.

Walking toward the door leading to the hall, she heard Captain Leeds say, "Let's do it as scheduled today. I'll assist you."

29

Arriving at her brother's bedside soon after his return from surgery, Emma found him groggy with his bandaged arm wrapped in ice packs to keep the swelling down. Awake enough to acknowledge her presence through half-opened eyes, he glanced at Wolfe standing beside her, who nodded. "Everything went well," Wolfe said. "We should know in a few days about your fingers."

All nurse, Emma added, "Now's the time to rest and recover from the operation. Too soon you'll face Juan, who will insist upon overseeing exercising your appendage."

"Listen to her," muttered Edmund, closing his eyes. "Controlling my life already. Next, she'll be managing my musical career as well as the rest of my life."

"Seems to me you need lots of sisterly advice. Besides, I have to make up for the years I wasn't around to keep you in line."

"Did you two always go at it this way?" interjected Wolfe. "Not having had a sibling, I guess I have much to learn about sibling squabbling."

"Who said we're squabbling? This is old-fashioned needling to keep life interesting. You better get used to it if you're going to be my husband."

Opening one eye, Edmund winked at Wolfe. "Did you hear that? She's forewarned you that she's planning to keep you on your toes every moment. Better think about that before you say 'I do.'"

Hearing footsteps, Emma turned. "Juan, he's out of surgery."

"I heard that. I'm here to talk to the doc about how soon I can start working on his arm, especially the fingers."

"Well, you'll have to wait until the bandages come off."

"Sure enough, but I need him on his feet and walking as well as exercising the other arm. Violin playing is a two-armed job," Juan said, smiling self-satisfied with his snappy response.

Looking up at the ceiling, Wolfe shook his head. "You're so alike—hard headed, pushy, and clannish." Gazing fondly at Emma, he started to leave but first told her, "After supper tonight, have him sit up on the side of his bed. Tomorrow, you can see how he tolerates standing up, but no walking until I okay it." With that, Wolfe left the ward chuckling to himself.

Emma and Juan exchanged knowing glances as they watched his departure. "He's recovered, at least for the time being," remarked Juan. "Do you think it will last?"

"Who knows, but getting him back helping patients certainly got him out of his rocking chair. I don't know about his nightmares, though. I'm hopeful that the recurrence of his tortured dreams will be minimal and cease completely."

"The need to help others often cures self-imposed phobias. That's the case even with animals," commented Juan, following Emma as they exited the ward.

Days later, Emma and Wolfe observed her brother chatting with other patients on his ward, many of them amputees. Depending upon the soldier he talked to, he either joked with them or listened to their fears. He often spoke in a stage whisper, displaying a sober face. "Lucky me, I'm in the minority here, not an amputee." That was followed by loud boos and bandaged arm and leg stumps waving in the air.

"Your brother has a real knack of raising patients' spirits," confided Wolfe. "I'm learning different bedside techniques from him."

"These men need personalized tender understanding so they can confront their loved ones back home. What they're facing isn't going to be easy," Emma confided.

"I know," said Wolfe. "And I know that goes for me too. It hasn't been easy on you seeing me isolate myself as I grappled with my memories. Thank goodness the desire to heal Edmund brought me out of my obsessive compulsions."

As Edmund headed back toward his bed, Emma and Wolfe followed him, noticing how he cradled his left arm with the right. "Is the arm hurting you?" asked Wolfe. "I see you're holding it as if it is."

"Yes, it hurts. Perhaps I should go back to using the sling."

"Well, let's have a look. Lay back and we'll take a look."

Emma, with Wolfe's help, began to cut away at the gauze bandage. He examined the hand and arm, asking as he touched various parts, "Does this hurt?" Edmund grimaced when Wolfe touched several places on his wrist. "Has your wrist always hurt like this or didn't you notice?"

"At first it was just a dull pain that I ignored, thinking it was just part of the healing but in the last day or so the pain has become constant."

Looking up at Emma, Wolfe asked, "Do you think you can locate Captain Leeds? I need to consult with him while the wrist is unwrapped. He'll need to see it."

"I'll go find him." Turning, Emma quickly set off.

Emma straightened the sheets and blanket on her brother's bed as she waited for him to return from surgery. Glancing at his violin case nearby, she couldn't resist the temptation to look at the instrument. As she lifted the violin from its case, a beaded neckless fell from the cloth around the violin, a rosary. *What's Edmund doing with a rosary,* she wondered. *We are not Catholic.* Holding the string of fifty beads with a cross at the end brought back the words of the "Hail Mary," which she had memorized years ago in Catholic school. As she fingered the rosary, she felt a peaceful shiver run clear to her toes. Automatically, her fingers slipped from bead to bead as she recited in her head the words she'd learned long ago. She stopped after each tenth bead knowing she was supposed to say something special but, having forgotten, said "Thank you, Lord." As a Protestant who'd been educated in a Catholic school, prayer didn't come naturally to her, but saying the rosary did. Chuckling to herself, she reflected on winning the award in her class for being the first to memorize the Stations of the Cross before all her Catholic classmates.

"May I join you?" interrupted Juan, slipping in beside her. "I heard Edmund is in surgery again. What happened?"

Hugging him, Emma allowed her grief to bubble onto his shoulder. She felt his warm comforting arms embrace her. No words were necessary as Juan gently held her close, his comfort spreading to her body. They stood there as one until Emma reached up to dry the moisture from her eyes. Pulling away, she smiled wanly and stepped back.

"Is that a rosary in your hand? I thought you were an Episcopalian?"

"I am, but I wanted to pray while I waited for Edmund to return from surgery. I found this rosary in his violin case. Saying the rosary came sort of naturally."

Juan reached out and kissed the hand holding the rosary. "I'm certain God listens to prayers in every form and in any language. All will be well. Wolfe's the best surgeon here and with Captain Leeds's assistance, Edmund's hand shall be saved. God hears you."

The two kept each other company as they paced back and forth in the ward, Emma's steps short and soundless alongside Juan's clipping riding-boot heels. Occasionally they stopped, turned to face each other, glanced at their watches, and continued pacing. Occasionally someone passed them, nodded, and went on their way. Finally, Wolfe and Captain Leeds emerged through the door. Emma scrutinized first one face and then the other in hopes of learning how the surgery went.

"He's come through fine," announced Captain Leeds, "But it's going to be a long time before we know how much use he'll have of his fingers."

"We did what we could," said Wolfe. "The infection had spread but I think we saved the hand. I'm sorry, Emma, he may not be able to play his violin. You'll have to be ready for that possibility."

30

Emma, Wolfe, and Juan encircled Edmund, voicing "goodbyes" as he waited his turn to climb into the ambulance delivering him to the train station, then on to the port where he'd depart for home. His hand, encased in a plaster-of-Paris cast up to the elbow, nested in a sling around his neck as he clutched his violin case in the other. On his back he carried his knapsack. He felt ridiculous waiting among those without legs and sightless. He was perfectly capable of climbing aboard himself but the attending nurse wouldn't allow it.

"We'll be back home soon to celebrate the end of the war. The Huns can't hold out much longer," Emma whispered as she gave her brother a kiss on his cheek. "Remember, Jamie and Mama will pick you up in Denver after your discharge."

Distracted but eager to be on his way, her brother looked around at the others traveling with him for a familiar face. Emma hoped he'd heard what she'd said. Since the second surgery, Edmund had been having a difficult time remembering facts. Wolfe assured her that as time passed, his memory should get better, especially if he regained enough of his finger dexterity to play his beloved violin. It had been three weeks since the second surgery and, for safety sake, the cast was left on, at least until he reached Denver.

As the ambulance drove away, Emma turned to Wolfe. "Thank goodness he's homeward bound. Between Mama and Jamie, they'll jolly him out of his funk. I've written Mama about his hand, suggesting she introduce him to one-handed piano pieces."

The three walked toward the hospital entrance. "I hear we have a medical staff meeting this afternoon concerning the pandemic we face," said Wolfe. "Are you included in it, Juan?"

"No, I have to hurry back to see about some kind of outbreak among the livestock. I'm just hoping it isn't too serious. The size of our fresh meet supply is depleted at the moment. Although we've decimated the German Navy, they still have enough clout to interrupt our food supply both from home and across the English Channel."

"Even the English people are feeling the shortage. Malnutrition is rampant there, just as it is here among our troops and the French people," commented Wolfe. "And we're short of certain medical supplies."

The hospital doctors and nurses, including Emma and Wolfe, sat listening as the director of the hospital announced a possible epidemic of a new flu virus and how they were going to handle the outbreak. Everyone faced handling the influenza with little scientific knowledge except that, if not treated quickly, they knew the virus resulted in pneumonia. The younger the patient, the better the chance to survive. It was puzzling. Now called the Spanish flu, no vaccine existed against it. The development of a vaccine, placed on a fast track, showed little progress because of scientific disagreement between laboratories in the States.

Turning to Wolfe, Emma said, "I'm glad Edmund is safely on his way back home."

"Don't be so sure. I've heard that at Fort Riley, Kansas, there's a full-blown pandemic. Let's just hope he is sent straight to Denver."

"Wasn't it Fort Riley where Juan was stationed before being sent overseas?" asked Emma.

"Yes, I believe you're right. The Veterinary Corps does have a unit there."

Returning to the serious subject of the flu, Emma asked, "Do they have any idea how it is spread?"

"I've heard overcrowding, malnourishment, and poor hygiene all of which our troops face here, contribute."

As they walked out of the meeting, Emma asked Wolfe in a whisper, "But some do survive, don't they?"

"Yes. The theory I've heard is that it has something to do with each person's immune system."

"Whatever," said Emma as they went their separate ways. "I hope we're both immune."

With her brother heading home and Wolfe returning to full-time duty, Emma found herself back at the field hospital near the front. Thomas the Tom greeted her with enthusiasm, wrapping himself around her legs and meowing as she unpacked. The tent had an earthy unclean smell since the former muddy grounds around it had dried to dust so unlike the dank musty smell when she'd departed. She noticed laundry hung without clothespins had slipped to the floor.

After stowing her garments away and placing her duffle bag under her cot, she smiled as Thomas jumped up on the now vacant bed and settled to nap. "Whose bed did you sleep on while I was gone?" she asked.

A voice behind her said, "He shared his furry self with everyone, depending on the work shift we had. Welcome back, Emma."

Turning, Emma faced Bev. "Thanks. It's great to be back. How's it been?"

Sitting on the corner of the adjacent cot, Bev brushed back a few strands of hair from her face. "I don't know if you want to know. First, it's been bitter cold. Then, the push to end this fight has increased the use of gas by the Germans. Our beds are filled with gassed soldiers, and a number of the nurses were affected too. We're working longer hours. Everyone's exhausted. So you are a welcome sight."

Giving Bev's hand a squeeze, Emma said, "I'm glad to be back too," and tilting her head toward Thomas, added, "And I see our four-legged male occupant of the tent has kept it free of vermin."

"Yes, he has. Did you notice how fat he's gotten?!"

Emma chuckled as she rose from the bed and leaned over to give the cat a pat. "Boy-son, you are the best. How I missed you while I was at the base hospital, not as pest controller, but as my personal psychologist."

"Guess it was a scary time for you, according to Juan."

"Yes, it was at first. Out here we don't see much of how the constant bombardment of the trenches affects the men. Being shell shocked is mystifying ... even the doctors don't know what to say or think, except to treat it with skepticism. Hopefully, when the men are away from the constant artillery noise, the nightmares will go away. It some cases it works but not for everyone. I'm very lucky. My fiancé has recovered, but we'll just have to wait and see."

"Well, I better get some shut-eye, or I won't be ready for my next shift," said Bev, heading for her cot. Then she looked over her shoulder and said, "Don't wait too long to go for supper. The food disappears pretty fast these days and there isn't much of it."

31

Emma watched as one of the German prisoners of war entered the ward to tend the fire. He wore a green uniform stamped in the front and back with the letters P.G., identifying him as a German prisoner. Most POW's assigned to the clinic were young, under the age of eighteen, and guarded by an American carrying a rifle. One of the prisoners Emma grew fond of seeing was fifteen-year-old Fritz, who came in twice each night to replenish the fuel in the wards' pop-bellied stove. His guard was a poker-faced, no-nonsense older soldier who stood rigidly at the door while Fritz did his job. When finished, Fritz stood in front of the guard, pressed one of his buttons on his uniform with a finger and laughingly said, "Ready," after which he'd turn, leaving the ward, followed by the guard.

One morning, after a twelve-hour duty stint, Emma dropped down at a table with others coming off duty. She glanced with little relish at a tiny mound of scrambled egg and cold toast on her plate. Nodding to Peggy, she reached for her black coffee as Peggy said, "No appetite? Me neither," shoving her untouched tray away.

Emma gave Peggy a weak smile, picking at her egg on the plate. "We should be glad we have something to eat. I hear at some stations they're down to toast and weak tea, no coffee."

"Mumm, you're probably right. I hope our doughboys finish this battle with the Huns quickly so we can head home."

Jerked upright, Emma realized her head had almost taken a nosedive into her food. She'd fallen asleep without answering

Peggy. Embarrassed, she looked around to see if anyone had noticed. Returning her tray, she stumbled out of the mess hall.

Thomas met her at the door of the quarters and escorted her to her cot as if she didn't know the way. Too tired to undress, she crawled under the covers, curling around the warm body of Thomas, who'd jumped onto the bed. Stroking the soft warm purring creature, Emma closed her eyes, but the sleep she'd fought during breakfast abandoned her. Fondling the furry body curled at her side, she said, "Billy, one of the patients who died tonight, Thomas, was too young to have an Adam's apple. A bullet went through his jaw and he couldn't even cry out. His deep blue eyes pleaded for help and I could do nothing but whisper comforting words to him. Major Pearson, the dentist, wired his jaw shut to heal but I think the wound in his chest did him in. Oh, Thomas, he was so young! He didn't even have a chance at life."

Emma wept into the short-haired tabby's fur, who purred and bumped his head against her. His wet pink nose reached up, touching her lower jaw as his tail rhythmically thumped her hip. Eventually, her crying ceased, and her hand relaxed on her companion's coat.

She struggled up from her fetal position, warm but groggy with eyelids stuck together. What time was it? What had awakened her? Fumbling to use her sleeve to clear the crustiness from her eyes, Emma recognized the voices of the day-shift nurses entering. Soft afternoon light from the doorway outlined them. Standing, she shivered as she slipped on her shoes and began searching for a clean uniform to wear. Shaking as she changed uniforms, she glanced at the lump on her covers where Thomas lay snug and warm. How she wished she could join him.

As Allie walked toward Emma, she asked, "Did you get enough rest? You looked pretty beat this morning at breakfast."

Giving a nod, Emma quickly straightened her sweater, which

in haste she'd buttoned wrong. Suddenly she felt hungry. *And why shouldn't I*, she thought. *I missed a meal.* "What's for dinner?" She asked in passing Peggy's cot space.

Looking up from the letter she was reading, Peggy shrugged, "Same old thing I think."

As Emma continued toward the door, Jackie stopped her. Guiding her into a corner, she said, "Think you should know that we got our first patient with the Spanish flu. He's been isolated but I hear it is really contagious."

Bobbing her head, Emma headed out after grabbing a helmet and a mask. Settling down with her coffee, she concentrated on satisfying her stomach, disregarding what her shift would bring.

Upon entering the first ward, Emma stood for a moment to allow her eyes to adjust to the darkness. There was only one electric light over a table in the center of the room that was surrounded by high screens over which blankets had been placed. The space created was known as the "nurses' dugout." Here's where she and the other nurses on night duty sat writing their reports. If a patient needed help, a kerosene lantern shaded by a dark blue gingham cloth was carried to the patient's bedside.

The second ward, dark like the first but without a nurses' dugout, although still having but one electric light, was abuzz with orderlies cleaning up and remaking the beds in anticipation of the next onslaught of patients from the front. The ward had already been emptied, as the patients were on their way to a general hospital. Emma busied herself in the supply office setting to rights the various bottles of medicine the doctors used, noting that they needed more morphine. As she put in place the last drugs, she heard the commotion of stretcher bearers entering the ward. Hurrying out, she began to direct each to a cot. Soon, all the beds were occupied by dirty and wounded men. The orderlies immediately set to work stripping the men of their uniforms and bandages, then washed their bodies as best they could so the doctors could decide what procedures were necessary. Keeping her mind impassive for fear of caving in at the horror around, Emma watched as the doctors removed bullets or pieces of shrapnel from wounds, wrapping them in gauze and tying them to the wrists of the patient so at the next hospital they'd know what had been removed.

Bleary-eyed and bone-tired, Emma headed to her quarters after eating a boiled egg and a strip of bacon along with a portion of French bread, but no butter since there wasn't any. It had been the best breakfast ever. Thomas waited at the door to escort her straight to her bed. Her breath vaporized as she slipped from her uniform into her woolen pajamas. Grabbing her woolen "wounded-foot socks," the gift of the knitting ladies back home made especially for men who only had a stump for a leg, minus the heel or toe, she put them on her feet, tucking her pajamas into them. She wound a scarf around her neck and slid in beside Thomas, welcoming the warm spot he'd created. Snuggling down, she wished she hadn't given her woolen sleeping bag to Juan.

32

Emma felt an arm under her shoulders lifting her up; then the edge of a glass touched her lips as a voice said, "Take a sip, one sip for me." Where was she? She tried to open her eyes but her lids were uncooperative. Her head screamed torture. Pain griped every bone in her body. Coughing ripped her body; it didn't stop. She couldn't breathe! Reddish liquid erupted from her mouth, gagging her. A cloth wiped her lips and chin. She felt her head lowered. She jerked, thrashing about and coughing, secreting more rosy fluid from her nose and mouth.

The nurse beside the bed turned to the doctor. "Isn't there anything we can do to stop this?"

"I'm afraid not. We need to keep her as calm as possible. Keep trying to get water into her."

Walking from the room, both doctor and nurse removed their face masks. "Shouldn't we let her fiancé know? He's here at the hospital."

Turning toward the nurse, the doctor nodded. "Yes, he should be told. I'm afraid we may lose this one. They waited too long before transporting her." Walking to the end of the ward, he washed his hands and arms.

Wolfe's taste buds and stomach alerted him that it was long past time for dinner. He hurried from the ward, stopping upon hearing his name called.

"Captain Gabel? Sir, I've got a message for you."

Wolfe tuned to face the redheaded ward nurse running toward him. "You are to report to Major Jackson's office immediately."

"Thanks." Puzzled as to why the major wished to see him, Wolfe grudgingly turned in the opposite direction of the mess hall. He rolled his tongue around his teeth thinking of the meal he was missing. Taking the stairs two at a time, he reached the second floor of the hospital leading to the major's office. The door was open, so he poked his head in. "You wanted to see me, Sir?"

"Come in, Captain. Close the door, please."

Wolfe stood at attention. Apparently, this was serious since he hadn't been asked to sit. What he could have done wrong escaped him. He hadn't as yet asked for leave to visit Emma, so it couldn't be concerning his request for one. His surgeries had gone well; he hadn't lost a patient. One knee buckled and shook, a nervous habit that he'd picked up since returning from being behind enemy lines.

"Captain, may I call you Wolfe?" asked the Major, getting up from his chair.

Looking straight at his superior, Wolfe wondered why the change in tone from military to personal? As he watched him walk around his desk, his anxiety increased.

"Last night, with the transport from the front, a nurse by the name of Emma Roeder arrived. I understand you two are engaged."

"Yes, Sir, we are." answered Wolfe, puzzled. Why did his superior make it his duty to inform him of Emma's arrival on post?

"Wolfe, I'm afraid Emma has contracted the Spanish flu."

In a strangled voice Wolfe asked, "Where is she?"

―――◇―――

Throwing his fouled gown into the laundry basket beside the door, Wolfe grabbed a clean gown and mask. As he nibbled on a slice of bread and gulped coffee left for him on a cart in the hall, he donned the sanitary clothing and new gloves as he reentered Emma's room.

She looked like a limp sack thrown onto the bed. With Wolfe's holding her in a sitting position during the last few hours, her thrashing about lessened. Fortunately, she wasn't coughing as frequently, and her nosebleeds had ceased.

Wolfe walked to the bed and, lifting Emma up into a sitting position, he settled himself beside her so he held her in his arms, a position he'd discovered helped stop her twitching and calmed her. Cuddling her close, Wolfe whispered, "You're going to get better. Breathe for me, for us. We've got so much ahead of us. Soon, we'll be headed back to Santa Fe. Remember, Edmund has been found. You want to hear him play his violin, don't you? You want to play your violin. Sweetheart, open your eyes for me." Wolfe looked at her gaunt face. "Blink those long eyelashes for me, darling, so I know you hear me." Sensing a cough, he tightened his arms around her, snuffing out a full-blown hacking. "There, you see? Together we can fight this terrible flu."

"How's she doing?" asked Juan, entering the room draped in a white gown and mask. "I came as soon as I heard."

Wolfe turned toward Juan, acknowledging his presence as he held Emma fighting a cough. "Better, I think, but delirious. She's in terrible pain."

Juan started toward the bed but was stopped by Wolfe's signal to stay back. "Isn't there something I can do?" he asked.

"Nothing," answered Wolfe, turning back toward Emma. "We're fighting this flu without the benefit of scientific knowledge. They're working at isolating the virus but so far with no success. There's no antidotes as yet. It's like the Black Plague, killing so mysteriously." Resettling his position next to Emma, he added, "You remember during our younger college days discussing medicine as an art as well as a science? Well, here's the art part and it's scary when it's a loved one who's affected."

"I too wish we had more scientific insight into the cause," commented Juan. "Since there's little I can do here, I'll be on my way. Help Emma get better and tell her I stopped by. You get our girl well, now, or I'll haunt you for the rest of your life. You can count on it," remarked Juan, scowling at Wolfe as he left.

Wolfe rejoiced as days went by and his grubby gowns changed from body fluid stained to broth and tea smudged. Emma was recovering. Her coughing had all but stopped. Her eyes, although lacking in brilliance, were focused and followed him as he moved. Her speech was halting and several decibels lower than normal. Weak, she required lots of rest to recuperate fully. She'd won her battle with the Spanish flu except for a persistent sore throat.

Juan made a surprise visit one Sunday, bringing her a bouquet of red roses along with a box of chocolates purchased at the post exchange in Paris, the only place such luxuries were available. He was off on a mission into enemy territory at the request of the Germans to rescue stray Lipizzan horses that were near starvation. Excited about his orders, Juan could hardly talk about anything else. Cold weather had been gripping Europe for several months, but Juan had confidence that he and his Navajo crew would find the stray horses and bring them back to Quartier Margueritte, where they'd be cared for until they could be returned.

Considered free of the Spanish flu but lacking energy, Emma was given her "Ds," a designation that she was to be sent home. Until such time as transportation was available, she was sent to an infirmary near Paris. She and Wolfe made plans for a future long-overdue holiday together once they could coordinate their leaves.

She was finally called to appear before the Classification Board as part of scheduling her return home. At the hearing, Emma learned that she'd been diagnosed with "nervousness" interpreted as goldbricking rather than being sick because of her sore throat. She couldn't let this one stand on her discharge record, so she heatedly objected. A female doctor on the board, checking into Emma's record, discovered that she in fact had a throat problem and continued fatigue resulting from her bout with Spanish flu. It wasn't goldbricking as the male doctor erroneously contended. Her discharge was corrected, and Emma would sail for home with a clean record of service to her country.

Victory came on the eleventh hour of the eleventh day of the eleventh month in 1918. Emma wasn't in Paris to see the streets lined with German tanks, machine guns, cannons, and airplanes. Nor did she see the thousands of German helmets placed in symmetrical rows on protective sheds over French statues. She was in Nice, staying at the Hotel Grimaldi, sharing a room with Maddie, while Wolfe and Kurt were in another. The two couples looked forward to exploring Monaco and doing some hiking in the surrounding mountains.

33

Emma along with three other nurses settled into their assigned cabin on the SS *Rijndam*. It was déjà vu. Anticipation of the ocean trip home tickled her imagination, as did the thought of seeing New York City without the marching down Fifth Avenue. This trip would be different from the one over to France.

As she stowed her bag under the lower berth along with her companions', Emma smiled to herself while looking at the upper bunks knowing that she'd probably occupy one since she was one of the shortest in stature. Sighing, she accepted the eventuality. The voyage wouldn't be as scary as the one over because there'd be no worry of seasickness or fear of being thrown out of her bunk caused by the ship's zigzagging maneuvering to avoid submarine attacks. The world was at peace. This trip would be a piece of cake.

"Come on, let's go wave *ave atque vale,* farewell to France. We're going home never to return," laughed her roommates, pulling her out the door.

Standing on the deck, one hand resting on the railing, Emma waved to the cheering crowd that watched as the gang plank was withdrawn. Scanning the faces, she didn't find one she recognized but how nice it was departing the port under a clear blue sky in the full warm sunshine rather than sneaking out under the dark of night for fear of U-boats, enemy ships, or submarines as they had to upon leaving New York City. The vessel's whistle gave several toots as it moved away from the dock, cheered by hands waving farewell. The somber ship's captain in his starched white uniform stood observing a local French-licensed pilot maneuver the ship from the port into the open channel before turning the wheel over to the naval officer beside him. A few passengers who lingered on deck watched as the pilot climbed down to his waiting boat to return ashore until another vessel required his services.

In the dining hall, passengers congregated for instructions on the proper procedure for putting on life jackets, a drill experienced previously on the trip over. To the annoyance of the person giving the instruction, the troops continued their gleeful jabbering until the loud speaker burst forth, "Attention!"

"This drill may save your life, so pay attention. Although we don't have to worry about the Germans anymore, there can be other incidents at sea that would require knowing how to save yourself. Please put your life jacket on and wait for it to be checked."

Low muttering resumed around Emma, who slipped into her own jacket before reaching across to the person facing her to untwist her jacket so she could slip her arm through the armhole. Time passed before they were all checked. The crowd became impatient as the heat from the throng increased. Beads of perspiration trickled down the center of Emma's back and her legs shook. *Don't faint*, she reminded herself. *Nurses don't faint.* Just as she was about to grab hold of the person next to her for support, the crewman arrived to check the life jackets.

"Okay, you're ready. Follow me to your lifeboat station out on deck."

Emma inhaled a deep breath of fresh air as she walked onto the open deck. It revived her. Her group followed their guide around and down a set of stairs until they stopped in front of one of the many small boats hanging over the side of the ship.

"This is your lifeboat station, station M. If you hear five long blasts on the ship's horn and repeated over and over, grab your life jacket and double time it to this lifeboat station. Wait until I arrive to give you directions to proceed. Climb into the boat when I tell you to, not before."

"Will we all fit in that boat? It looks too small for all of us," challenged a man.

"Yes, you'll all fit. The men will take the oars unless we need help from the ladies. Any questions?"

Looking around, Emma wondered if the women would go before the men but decided not to ask such a trivial question since they were all soldiers who'd faced the Huns together and won. With no more questions, they were dismissed.

Supper that night was a raucous affair with a feast of roast beef, Yorkshire pudding with brown gravy, three different vegetables, hot rolls, and triple-layered chocolate cake but no wine. *What an affront, since we just left France,* thought Emma. Laughter bubbled around every table with shared jokes and teasing. Best of all, the ship was lit up like a Christmas tree, no need to hide the victor's candle under a coverlet. They'd won the war.

Worn out from the excitement of boarding the ship carrying them home and a comfortable, full feeling in her tummy, Emma snuggled into her top bunk, falling asleep soon after pulling her blanket around her shoulders. Her roommates moved around, slipping into their pajamas quietly, fluffing pillows, hanging up uniforms, and brushing their teeth before they too fell asleep to the faint sound of the throbbing ship's motors.

Emma awoke to light streaming through the porthole, producing a rainbow of colors above her. She sat up abruptly, hitting her head on the low ceiling. Falling back on her pillow, her head hurting, she couldn't catch her breath. Where was she? Oh, yes, back on a troop ship headed home! As she touched her smarting head, she stretched her cramped legs out as far as she could in her bunk, ordering herself to relax and take a deep breath.

Then she heard, "Good morning, guys. Up and at 'em! First one to the john gets it."

Hearing the door slam and the flush of the commode, Emma slid sidewise and slithered off the bunk and onto the floor. She wanted to be next in line. Tomorrow she'd be first, she told herself as she gathered her towel, washcloth, and soap dish. The other two roommates appeared sound asleep, or at least they hadn't been roused by the noise, so she'd have time for a shower. Leaning against the wall waiting, she recalled the long waits to shower on the trip over. No showering had been allowed at night because of blackout restrictions as they'd sailed the Atlantic. Not assigned staterooms on that trip, the forty or so women shared a small communal bathing and sleeping area. Their present facility was pure luxury compared to that.

Whereas the days crossing the ocean to Europe in the fall of 1917 crawled at a snail's pace, the trip back home in 1919 seemed to fly by. Women who'd volunteered to serve in France for the YWCA, the Salvation Army, or as civilian workers for the American Expeditionary Force organized daily pastimes aboard ship, besides the daily morning calisthenics required of the men. These included talent shows, dances, games, concerts, races, and other competitions that occupied all the free spaces aboard the ship. The ship's library boxes were popular because they contained all the recently published best-selling books people missed while in France.

One morning, close to the end of their trip, Emma came upon a lone young woman gazing across the wide expanse of ocean toward another vessel traveling in their convoy. Placing a hand on the railing to maintain her balance, Emma leaned over to watch their ship cut through the water, leaving small waves. "It's nice to be going home, isn't it?"

Expecting to see a cheery face turn her way, Emma was taken

aback to see a puffy-faced, red-eyed youngish girl looking at her. Emma produced a handkerchief, placing it in the girl's hand, and wrapped an arm around the young woman's shoulder. For several moments, Emma just held the grieving girl close, saying nothing.

Soon, the tears were replaced by body shutters and hiccups. The girl freed herself from Emma's grasp, saying, "Thank you, I'll be okay now."

"Are you sure you're better now?" Holding out her hand, she added, "I'm Emma."

Interrupted by a loud hiccup, they shook hands. "I'm Peg."

"Glad to meet you, Peg. Whatever brought on your tears now that we're on our way home to the States? You should be happy!"

Sniffling, Peg looked over at her sympathizer and then down before answering. "I know, but I can't help it. My fiancé was to be on this ship until he was hospitalized with pneumonia. They wouldn't let me stay with him but insisted I go home."

"I bet he'll be on the next available ship home. He still has his D papers, so just as soon as he recovers, he'll be on his way."

Glancing at Emma's uniform, Peg nodded as she wiped a few stray tears from her cheeks. "You're a nurse, aren't you?"

"Yes."

"Well, how serious is pneumonia when a person coughs up colored fluid and his face has a bluish cast?"

Trying to keep her face expressionless, Emma asked, "Did you observe those symptoms?"

"Yes, and he had brown spots over his cheek bones that I'd never noticed before."

"Peg, I'm only a nurse. If the doctor diagnosed his condition as pneumonia, I'm certain it is. With good care, he'll recover and rejoin you soon. He may even reach Newport News before we do."

Suddenly, an arm latched onto Emma's. "Come join us for coffee," said one of her roommates walking by.

Glad to have an excuse to leave Peg, who unintentionally disclosed to her that her boyfriend probably had contracted the influenza virus, Emma joined her roomy.

"What was bothering the girl you were talking to, Emma?"

Glancing around the table where they sat with coffee and donuts, Emma lowered her voice. "She was telling me about her boyfriend, who was supposed to be on this ship with her but ended up in the hospital. From her description of his symptoms, I think he may have the Spanish flu rather pneumonia, as she was told."

"Oh, how awful!"

"Mother wrote me that the flu has been spreading all around the Army camps at home among the recruits. She warned me to be extra careful because of so many dying from it," said Nell, the roommate who also had the privilege of sleeping with her nose to the ceiling like Emma.

"In my last letter from home, Dad told me my uncle was the only one in his barracks to survive the flu," added Hettie, the early-bird roommate.

"This flu is awful—my chum from nursing school lost her fiancé to it. He was fine one day and gone two days later. He was a jeweler in our small Wyoming town, the only victim for miles around according to the doctor."

This last comment from Hettie ended further discussion. All fell silent, deep in thought about what they'd heard. What kind of epidemic would they face upon reaching home?

Speaking softly, Sally, from New Jersey, said, "Before leaving France, I overheard the Chief Nurse saying that at Camp Devens in my home state, the wards are overflowing. They are so short of doctors and nurses that the Army is bringing in civilians to help out."

"Let's hope that by the time we arrive stateside, this epidemic has subsided and the Army won't need us." Catching the eye of each girl, Emma added, "All of us are looking forward to being discharged so we can get back to our civilian lives."

"We agree, Emma," cheered the girls, clinking their coffee cups together in a toast. "Here's to getting discharged upon landing in good old U S of A!"

34

As Emma stepped off the gangplank onto American soil for the first time in two years, she considered doing a tap dance but instead followed the other nurses. Disappointed that her discharge from the Army Nurse Corps had been delayed, it hardly registered with her where the bus was taking them. Thinking that they'd end up at a New York City hotel, she looked forward to a warm bath, a full-sized bed, and a meal at a café rather than mess hall fare. When the bus stopped, she saw rows of barracks, one marked "receiving." They were being quarantined. What a shock!

Discharge wouldn't happen even after their clean bill of health, they discovered. The Spanish flu pandemic filled civilian as well as military hospitals, creating a grave shortage of medical staff. The nurses learned that they would be assigned to military hospitals around New York and New Jersey wherever needed. They had no choice—orders had to be obeyed. Some were assigned as "floaters," meaning they'd work at several different hospitals in the area. Emma found herself assigned to only one ward, not a Spanish flu one, because of her perceived low resistance to it.

Arriving at her duty station, she began walking down the aisle of beds, glancing from side to side. A broad smile creased her face as she looked into the grinning faces welcoming her. The patients assigned her were all her "pets" from France! These were the jolly and likable ones she'd never forgotten, all physically disabled, thus requiring special care.

The days passed quickly caring for her favorite patients.

They enjoyed all the foods they missed while in France: hot dogs, hamburgers, milkshakes, and real coffee. Daily afternoon treats of ice cream brought smiles to all, even the patients experiencing pain.

One such patient was O'Brian, a champion college boxer who was fitted with metal braces holding together what remained of his terribly mutilated face. A specially constructed contraption encircled his head above his eyebrows, with another encircling his lower jaw. Upright metal supports locked the two in place. He insisted only Emma feed him because he liked the way she poured his food through a funnel attached to tubing beside of his mouth. Emma noticed him having trouble sleeping and asked if there was something she could do to help.

"Well, I could sleep all right if I didn't have to keep one eye open all the time," he answered.

"Why must you keep one eye open?" asked Emma.

"Well, you see, I'm afraid someone will steal this contraption the dentist devised for me," pointing to his jaw brace. "Then what would I do?"

Wolfe arrived stateside within a month of Emma. To celebrate, they dined at the officers' club since he was confined to post until they were certain he didn't carry the Spanish flu bug. Emma looked forward to a pleasant reunion but when she met Wolfe, she realized something was wrong. *What could it be*, she wondered.

Holding Emma's hand, Wolfe told her that Juan completed his rescue of the Lipizzan horses and delivered them back to France, when the weather turned icy cold, making it impossible to complete their trip. He'd sheltered the horses in an abandoned barn and for the night sought refuge for himself in a nearby hut. He built a fire in the fireplace for warmth and snuggled into his woolen sleeping bag. In the morning, when he didn't appear, his troopers went searching for him and found him asphyxiated. An investigation showed that the chimney of the fireplace was completely blocked by small animals seeking warmth. With nowhere to go, the smoke from the fire filled the hut smothering Juan, too exhausted to awaken.

"NO!" screamed Emma. "No, not Juan!" she howled, rejecting Wolfe's outstretched embrace. Shaking her head as sobs racked her body, she shook off Wolfe's hands as he tried to comfort her.

"Emma, I'm so sorry," consoled Wolfe, reaching out to her.

"Stay away from me," she screamed. "Don't touch me," she spat, pulling away from his open arms.

Puzzled, Wolfe dropped his arms and watched her run from the club. He'd never seen her react this way. She'd never rejected any loving overtures of his before. Shoving his hands in his pockets, his face constrained, he shrugged and walked after her.

A knock at the door awakened her. "Emma, supper's ready."

Nudging Fiver off the bed, she threw her legs over the side and stood up. It was Saturday, the entire family would be there. How could she face everyone? Home a week, she'd isolated herself from all except Mama and Jamie. She hadn't even allowed Wolfe to visit. Oh, if she could only speak with Juan. He'd explain to her why she was acting the way she was; but Juan was gone, gone forever. Why?

Another knock at her door startled her. "Emma, it's Mama. May I come in?"

"Yes, of course," answered Emma, still sitting on her bed.

Now gray haired, but still with bright sparkling eyes and suntanned skin almost as dark as Spanish American Aunt Maria's, Mama entered. Taking a seat beside Emma on the bed, she said, "Fritz and Maria are here. They're anxious to see you. Won't you please have supper with us?"

"I'm trying," answered Emma. "But it's so hard." Flushed and red faced, she rubbed her eyes with her fists before accepting the handkerchief offered by Mama.

"Darling, I know it's difficult, but you must try." Patting Emma's hand, Mama shifted so she could put her arm around Emma's. "Didn't you realize how much you loved Juan?"

"No," squeaked Emma. "I thought of him as a brother like Edmund."

"Well, now you have Edmund. God took one and gave one back. You should be thankful, not moping about for Juan. He wouldn't want you to be like this."

Giving her mother a squeeze, Emma whispered, "I know, but I didn't even realize I loved him. He never knew how I felt." Raising her head so she looked at her mama, she asked, "What am I to do?"

"First of all, I believe Juan knew of your strong feelings toward him. He also knew you were attracted to Wolfe, not him." Sitting back from her daughter, Mama reached up and brushed the hair hanging over one eye. "You must do the honorable thing: be truthful with Wolfe. Talk to him about you not realizing how you felt about Juan until his death."

<hr />

Emma took the early afternoon train to Albuquerque. Several days ago, Wolfe invited her down for the weekend. Since his discharge from the Army, he'd taken a temporary position with a physician looking for a replacement interested in joining his practice.

As the train left the Santa Fe station, Emma couldn't help hoping to hear the solid heels of Juan's cowboy boots and his asking, "Is this seat vacant?" Glancing out the window at the passing adobe buildings and red chili strings hanging from the house vigas. With one finger she brushed a tear from under her eye.

"*Señorita*, is this seat vacant?" inquired a swarthy pleasant-faced man clad in a blue cotton shirt open at the neck revealing tufts of black hairs.

Jerked from her reverie, Emma gulped before indicating he was welcome. As he stretched to throw his Navajo blanket above, she couldn't help observed his muscular toned body. *He's a handsome one*, she thought to herself and then chastised herself for having such thoughts. How could she look at another man with her beloved Juan dead? But this man beside her reminded her of her Juan. Emma turned back to the window. She wanted to discourage any conversation.

"You going to Albuquerque or on to El Paso?" asked the person beside her whose voice carried a southwestern twang.

Turning, Emma replied, "Just to Albuquerque."

"Me too," smiled her seatmate turning, toward her. "I'm Michael. Most people call me plain Mike."

Nodding, she stammered, "Glad to meet you, Mike."

Emma tried to clear the vision of Juan's twinkling black eyes looking at her in place of Mike's. His scent was familiar. Taking another whiff, she tried to identify where she'd encountered it before. Nothing came to her. Glancing down, she noticed his cowboy boots appeared new. How odd! Sneaking another look at her seatmate, Emma felt a shiver go through her body.

Mike opened a brown paper-covered book and began reading. Emma frowned as she noticed it was a book of poetry. That's unusual for a cowboy, she thought; neither Juan nor Wolfe read poetry. Shrugging her shoulders, she turned toward the window seeking solace.

Closing his book, Mike looked over at the woman next to him. He sensed she would like to talk. Since the end of World War I he'd noticed the same desperate looks among returning veterans. Could this young woman be someone who'd faced and been part of that Great War? Clearing his throat, he turned so he could look at her while speaking. "By any chance, did you serve overseas in France during our recent war?"

Emma blanched as she turned to look at him. She noticed faint letters printed on his book, BIBLE. She answered a question with a question. "How did you know?"

"It was a hunch. A good one, I guess." Pausing for a second before continuing, he asked, "What did you do?"

"I was in the Army Nurse Corps."

"Are you still nursing?" he asked.

"No," answered Emma, distracted by perceiving it was Juan's scent she detected on this stranger. Her head began to spin. Her eyes misted over.

In a fog, she watched Mike reach for something at his neck. His hand brought out a silver cross on a chain. Absently he rubbed it, head bowed.

"Why not?"

Emma signed, "After seeing all the carnage in France, I, I can't go back into a ward or surgery. All those young lives lost or destroyed for what?"

"You seem like a dedicated nurse. You should never give up on a gift loaned you by our Lord. Are you telling me the truth about giving up nursing?"

Giving Mike an unsparing look, Emma hissed, "You don't know anything about me."

"Maybe not, but I know you'll lose your talent unless you make use of it. What a waste that would be."

Mike turned from her, his attention drawn to a crying baby several seats away. Emma looked toward the mother and child. When the baby's crying suddenly stopped, Mike shot to his feet, grabbed the child, and held it under the ribs and pushed. Suddenly, out popped a small object. The baby immediately took a breath and started crying.

After handing the child to its mother, Mike resumed his seat beside her. "That truly was a miracle. How did you know?"

Mike smiled but didn't' answer. He opened his brown paper-covered book and began to read.

Emma turned to watch the tumbleweeds scattering from the moving train. A quietness settled around her as a strange warmth embraced her. A slight tickle near her ear made her reach up and look over toward Mike. The seat was empty. Looking up and down the aisle, she saw no one. Only the faint scent of her seatmate remained. Facing the window, she smiled at a billowy cloud above, nodded, and whispered, "Thank you, Lord!" She had her answer for Wolfe.

35

The table they'd been seated at by the waiter wearing the traditional Mexican ruffled shirt was in a small inner room of the restaurant on the southwest corner of the Old Town's plaza. An all-time favorite from student nursing days, Emma felt comfortable and pleased that Wolfe remembered her love of Mexican food, especially since she knew he preferred German cuisine even after all those years in Santa Fe with her family.

She didn't have to glance at the menu to know what to order: a combination plate of all her favorites, plus extra guacamole. Looking over at Wolfe, she saw him flip to the "American" section of the menu, betting with herself that he'd order a well-done steak, along with fried potatoes and a salad. Wolfe also ordered fruit-juice cocktail minus the alcohol. They both indulged in the bowl of tortilla chips and salsa placed on the table for them while waiting their dinners.

As they raised their glasses, Wolfe toasted, "To our future, whatever it might bring."

Emma took a sip of her cocktail. Her heart, full of happy expectation when they arrived, had slipped a notch. What did he mean, "whatever it might bring"?

Stepping off the train, she'd been ready to tell him that she'd marry him, now glancing at his sober face, she wondered if he'd changed his mind.

"How's everything at home?" asked Wolfe, setting his glass down and reaching for a tortilla chip.

Putting her glass down, Emma spread her napkin on her lap before speaking. "Your Pa's off to Idaho to buy sheep for Fritz and Maria. Did you ever think he'd expand his talents into livestock buying?"

Chuckling, Wolfe moved slightly back in his chair. "No, but I'm never surprised at any challenge he takes up. I'll bet Fritz is pleased to have him as the new agent. Did Jamie go with him to Idaho to visit old friends?"

"No, my stepfather is busy breaking Edmund in as manager of the mercantile."

Shifting his feet as he spoke, Wolfe added, "I'm glad your brother has decided to take over the business after Jamie retires. That frees you to follow your own career path, doesn't it?"

Emma straightened in her chair, hands clasped in her lap as she looked across at her fiancé. Just as she was about to reply, the waiter arrived with their plates.

The house mariachi band appeared beside their table as they began eating. Could he be ready to brake off their engagement? She guessed he had every right to do so. Since learning of Juan's death, she had been terrible to him. He'd been so understanding and thoughtful. Could he forgive her? Peeking over at him, she found him intent on his meal. Had they lost their feelings for each other? It seemed so.

"Dr. Gabel, there's a phone call for you at our cashier's desk," interrupted their waiter.

As Emma waited for Wolfe to return from taking his call, she wondered what kind of emergency it could be, knowing surgeons often received such calls. It wasn't long before Wolfe returned to stand facing her. "I'm afraid I have to cut our dinner short. I'm needed at St. Joseph's. I'll drop you off at the hotel on the way."

Early the next morning, Emma set off for St. Joseph's Hospital, which was only a short distance away. She rather enjoyed taking the familiar walkway beneath the train tracks, turning north at the first corner near the high school, and walking several blocks to the red brick, two-story hospital on the corner. It looked the same as when she'd attended nursing school, very welcoming with its large shade trees and finely clipped green grass.

Emma readily found the cafeteria, settling down at an empty table with a cup of coffee and a donut, something she rarely indulged in at home. Looking around, she identified student nurses and members of patients' families. She watched as a doctor grabbed coffee and disappeared. The hospital setting calmed Emma, making her feel at home, something she'd been missing but hadn't realize it until now.

"Good morning. Glad to see you found your way here."

Emma looked up into a pair of weary, tired eyes. The blue gown Wolfe wore was wrinkled, indicating that he'd probably slept in it.

"Good morning to you too. Long night, huh?" said Emma, motioning for him to join her at the table. "Did the surgery go well last night?"

Rubbing his hand over his forehead and back through his rumpled hair, he answered, "Yeah, but a tough go most of the night. Sorry I left you in the lurch last night."

Reaching across the table, Emma took his free hand in hers. "You should know I understand. Don't worry. Are we going to have some time to talk today?"

"Of course. I have rounds this morning but how about lunch? Here would be the easiest for me."

Emma watched as Wolfe sipped his coffee. He appeared to be completely worn out and in need of sleep. "Lunch here would be wonderful. I'd like to visit with Sister Una this morning if she's available. I'll be fine as long as I don't miss the last train for Santa Fe."

Wolfe nodded and left the table, carrying his cup. His steps lagged, and he slouched slightly. Emma watched as he dragged himself away. *What happened to him*, she wondered. She'd never seen him so despondent. *Could her refusal of him since learning of Juan's death have caused this?* She hoped not.

Emma visited several other sisters along the way as she headed for Sister Una's office on the second floor. She'd made her mind up to see if there might be a vacancy in the teaching staff for her. Although she loved nursing, she didn't feel ready to return to floor duty and thought teaching might be a way to ease back into the real world. Knocking on Sister Una's door, Emma heard a cheerful "Come in."

"Oh, what a delightful surprise. I heard you were visiting the hospital and hoped you'd stop by," said Sister Una rising from behind her desk and moving with a swish to Emma, kissing both of her cheeks as Emma did in turn. "Come, sit down. Would you like some tea?"

"Thank you, no, I've already had enough coffee to float away," replied Emma settling herself in the chair facing Sister's desk. The same chair she had sat in long ago when she'd come to learn her fate after the first six-month trial period as a student nurse. Now, even after two years of nursing service at the front lines in France, she sat as fidgety as the first time in front of Sister Una.

"I hear you've experienced life at its best and at its worst. And your training served you well while with the Army Nurse Corps in France. We here at St. Joseph's Hospital are very proud of you."

"Thank you, Mother, but I don't feel like I did anything special, just my duty," replied Emma, bowing her head, her hands clasped tightly on her lap.

"I've heard that you've kept your fiancé at a distance since learning of Juan's untimely death. Is that correct?"

"Yes, I took Juan's death very hard." Looking at Sister Una, she added, "I suddenly felt a deep loss that I took as love for him."

"Did you talk to Wolfe about how you felt?"

Shaking her head, Emma said, "No, I rejected all his attempts to console me. I don't understand why I've hurt Wolfe the way I have."

"You saw many men die needlessly in France, didn't you? Juan's untimely death coming after the armistice shocked you. Your sense of justice came unhinged like Wolfe's did when he reverted inward after his experience behind the German lines. Can you see that what you've gone through is similar to what Wolfe has? A mental coping mechanism."

Emma stared into space until a flash of understanding came. "Why didn't I make the connection?!" Rising from the chair, she said, "Thank you, Sister. You've been of great help! See you later!"

Sister Una smiled to herself as she watched Emma rush out the door. Crossing herself, she looked heavenward saying, "Thank you, Lord, for giving me the right words to heal a very special woman."

Wolfe stood as Emma approached the table in the cafeteria where he'd waited. He'd taken a short nap after rounds so he felt ready to contend with any of Emma's many moods. He'd filled his tray with chili and rolls for them both. Time was of the essence, since Emma had spoken about getting back to Santa Fe today. He also had a surgery scheduled midafternoon.

"Mumm, the chili smells scrumptious," said Emma picking up her spoon. "I'm starved."

"Thought you'd like it. Our cook's the best, especially for lunches."

"Do you eat most of your meals here?" asked Emma.

"Yes, you know I only have one room close to the hospital. Don't need much more since I'm not there much." Glancing over at her, he watched to see what effect his remark had on her. A spark burst in his chest as he saw Emma wiggle her body like she had ants in her pants planning to pull a trick on him. *What was she up to?* he wondered.

"Are you interested in what I've been thinking?" asked Emma mysteriously.

"Yes, but first let me tell you my news. I—, I've accepted a position in Texas, San Antonio." Wolfe watched as Emma deflated like a balloon into a rag doll, her face contorted and covered by her hands.

"No, no, just as I was about to tell you …"

"Tell me what?"

Taking her hands away from her face, Emma threw her paper napkin down on the table and stood up. "Just as I was going to ask for forgiveness for rejecting you. I love you. I'm ready to marry you. I'm so sorry." Snatching her purse, she ran from him, unaware of all the questioning looks on people's faces around.

"Emma, wait!" cried Wolfe, following her. Reaching the hall outside the cafeteria, he looked in both directions. It was deserted. How could she disappear so quickly? Where could she have gone? Angry at himself for his impatience to tell her of his news rather than listening to hers first, he stumbled toward the hospital's screened-in porch area at the end of the hall where there were rocking chairs.

Pulling herself out of bed, Emma slipped into her work clothes. A week had passed since she returned from Albuquerque. With nothing else to do, she'd promised Jamie and her brother she'd take supplies out to the ranch for Fritz and Maria, who'd been under the weather for the last few days. While there she'd check on both to see if they needed more medical care than they'd been giving themselves.

Arriving at the ranch, Emma couldn't raise anyone, not even the hired hand, to help her unload the supplies into the barn. After unloading sacks, she entered the hacienda to see about Fritz and Maria. "I'm here! Where is everyone?" she called, finding no one in the great room. "Hello, where are you?" Puzzled, she stood in the middle of the room listening for sounds. Squeak, squeak ... Emma turned toward the sound of a door opening.

There in a Stetson hat, plaid shirt with bolo tie, jeans, and cowboy boots stood Wolfe. Before she could react, he said, "I accept your apology and ask that you accept mine." Stepping toward her, he continued, "Please, I should have listened to you first the other day before blurting out my news about the Texas job offer. I don't want to live anywhere without you." Moving toward her until he was only inches away from her, he put his hands on her shoulders. "I love you, always have. Please be my New Mexico gal and let me be your New Mexico guy?"

Emma stepped into his arms, knocking his Stetson to the floor and whispered, "Yes!" Laughing, she added, "But don't lose your head over this."

"No," he replied laughingly, "Just my heart."

Dear Reader

In the planning stages, *Gone to War* was visualized as a historical romance centering on Emma, a nurse; her fiancé, Wolfe, a doctor; and her childhood friend Juan, a veterinarian. The romance side of the novel became secondary as I researched the Army Nurse Corps. The social changes, especially for women, that have taken place over the past one hundred years is remarkable and requires recognition and celebrating.

Initially, I found few primary sources concerning World War I Army nurses, as they may reside in local historical museums or archives. Many published secondary sources, I discovered, contained conflicting news, misinformation, or ignored the subject altogether.

My research took me to the many early British publications, such as Vera Brittain's *Chronicle of Youth: The War Diary, 1913–1917* and Dorothea Crewdson's *Dorthea's War: A First World War Nurse Tells Her Story*. I began my U.S. research by reading *Nurses at the Front*, edited by Margaret R. Higonnet. Jennifer D. Keene's books on World War I provided me with a good overview of our participation in the war. Susan Zeiger's book *In Uncle Sam's Service: Women Workers with the American Expeditionary Force, 1917–1919* was enlightening. A recently published book by Matthew D. Tippen, *Turning Germans into Texans: World War I and the Assimilation and Survival of German Culture in Texas, 1900–1930*, gave insight into the prejudice against the German American population during the period. At the same time, I interviewed acquaintances whose female relatives had served overseas, spoke with visitors to the

World War I Museum in Kansas City while researching the archives there, reviewed the resources at the World War I Archives, and read my grandfather's personal log written during his lifetime when he'd captained a merchant ship from New York City to France carrying supplies.

Even before the book was contemplated, I'd been an avid reader of romance novels set during World War I and skeptical of the somewhat rosy picture presented because of my personal experience living with Army nurses during the Vietnam War. When I went to the World War I Archives in Kansas City, my suspicions were confirmed as I read through the letters of Alta Andrews Sharp to her mother during the two-year period she served in the Army Nurse Corps in France. My fictitious Emma story, as I'd already written, followed closely the experiences of Alta Sharp. My intuition had been correct.

Most of the incidents in the book are based on facts gleaned from my research but I have drawn from my own life experiences too, such as shell-shocked behavior, now identified as PTSD. After World War II, while my father was hospitalized at Fort Lewis, Washington, I visited shell-shocked patients who recuperated in rocking chairs on a screen porch in the hospital. I watched my own father suffer with "war's shock" caused by his days in the jungle of Burma. During the Vietnam War, I served in the Women's Army Corps at William Beaumont Hospital in El Paso, Texas. I lived in the nurses' quarters, ate at the hospital mess, and commanded a company of women who were nurses' aides and medical specialists. William Beaumont received seriously wounded patients directly from Vietnam. I've borrowed several of those vivid memories for the book.

Yes, I have taken some poetic liberties. Wolfe's capture and rescue by Juan is one. That's purely fictional. The wine cellar escape is an adaptation of a similar episode that took place during

World War II in France as told me by a friend. The Lipizzan horse rescue took place during World War II, not World War I. It was carried out to save the horses from being taken by the advancing Russian troops. I knew the leader of the American group that saved the horses.

The researching and writing of the book has been a marvelous experience. Personal memories, as well stories recounted by others, were remembered and brought to life. As I lived along with Emma the life of a World War I Army nurse, I began to appreciate the many struggles past generations faced and their achievements made that we today take for granted. May we never forget to be thankful for their sacrifices.

About the Author

Enid is very familiar with the Army Nurse Corps having first come in contact with army nurses when the family followed their army dentist father around camps during WW2. During the Viet Nam era war, Enid, an officer in the Women's Army Corps, served at William Beaumont General Army Hospital in El Paso, Texas, residing in the nurses' quarters and commanded a company of army practical nurses, and other enlisted women medical specialists. Not a nurse, Enid is a retired research librarian and teacher. She's published a research guide with Greenwood Press as well as written and self-published six other books. Gone to War is her sixth book based on historical events.

CPSIA information can be obtained
at www.ICGtesting.com
Printed in the USA
FFHW022038201118
49518065-53878FF